ROBERT DREWE

NED KELLY

PENGUIN BOOKS

PENGUIN BOOKS

Published by the Penguin Group

Penguin Group (USA) Inc., 375 Hudson Street, New York, New York 10014, U.S.A.
Penguin Books Ltd, 80 Strand, London WC2R 0RL, England
Penguin Books Australia Ltd, 250 Camberwell Road,
Camberwell, Victoria 3124, Australia
Penguin Books Canada Ltd, 10 Alcorn Avenue, Toronto, Ontario, Canada M4V 3B2
Penguin Books India (P) Ltd, 11 Community Centre,
Panchsheel Park, New Delhi – 110 017, India
Penguin Books (N.Z.) Ltd, Cnr Rosedale and Airborne Roads,
Albany, Auckland, New Zealand
Penguin Books (South Africa) (Pty) Ltd, 24 Sturdee Avenue,
Rosebank, Johannesburg 2196, South Africa

Penguin Books Ltd, Registered Offices:
80 Strand, London WC2R 0RL, England

First published in Australia as *Our Sunshine* by Pan Macmillan Australia Pty Ltd 1991
Published by Penguin Books Australia Ltd 2001
This edition published in the United States of America in Penguin Books 2003

1   3   5   7   9   10   8   6   4   2   ·

LIBRARY OF CONGRESS CATALOGING IN PUBLICATION DATA
Drewe, Robert, 1943–
[Our sunshine]
Ned Kelly / Robert Drewe.
p.   cm.
Originally published under title: Our sunshine.
ISBN 0 14 20.0315 8
1. Kelly, Ned, 1855–1880—Fiction.   2. Bushrangers—Fiction.
3. Australia—Fiction.   I. Title.
PR9619.3.D77O93 2003
823'.914—dc21   2002193129

Printed in the United States of America

Praise for *Ned Kelly*

"Robert Drewe's revisionary—and visionary—novel makes your heart thud."

—*Time Out London*

"This is a mesmerizing novel."

—*Times Literary Supplement*

"This book is addictive. Drewe's language is, as ever, astonishing, with every one of his sentences containing a shiver of exactness and immediacy."

—*New Statesman*

"A tour de force . . . A model of style and passion."

—*The Age*

"Drewe has performed a remarkable feat of literary sleight of hand . . . [*Ned Kelly*] is a marvelous book."

—*Sydney Morning Herald*

PENGUIN BOOKS

NED KELLY

Robert Drewe was born in Melbourne and grew up on the West Australian coast. His novels and short stories have been widely translated, won many national and international prizes, and been adapted for film, television, radio and the theater. He has also written plays, screenplays, journalism and film criticism, and edited two international anthologies of stories. He lives with his family on the central coast of New South Wales.

Also by Robert Drewe

Fiction
The Savage Crows
A Cry in the Jungle Bar
The Bodysurfers
Fortune
The Bay of Contented Men
The Drowner

Memoir
The Shark Net

Non-fiction
Walking Ella

Plays
South American Barbecue
The Bodysurfers: The Play

As Editor
The Penguin Book of the Beach
The Penguin Book of the City

For
James Fraser
and
Ray Lawrence

Myth is gossip grown old.

STANISLAW LEC

He stole my left ear. I took his right eye. He concealed fourteen of my teeth. I sewed up his lips. He stewed my behind. I turned his heart inside-out. He ate my liver. I drank his blood. War!

ELIAS CANETTI

No one is himself . . .

PAUL BOWLES

NED KELLY

FLARE

The lion is out of sorts. It's probably the smoke more than the human hubbub or the seesawing concertina music making it bark that deep and chilling moan and scrape its ribs along the bars of its wagon. You have to step close to see it – then hold your breath and heart still. Against every instinct, press your face up to the bars and peer into the ferocious meaty shadows. The bars are chipped and jungle-coloured, far too fragile-looking, with damp lion-fluff sticking to them. Balls of dusty lion-moult drift over the floor, too, among the odd bullock shin and lion dropping, and the lion pads through this muck with a fierce thin-hipped precision. Controlled panic. It hacks its moaning cough, it paces, it rubs its skin raw, but its paws never touch bone or turd.

From the pub's verandah he can catch a glimpse of the lion each time they throw another branch on the bonfire.

Now its tension has spread to the camel and four circus ponies. And to Mirth, dear Mirth, twitching and stamping on her tether in the saplings behind the inn. A mangy old lion, but not often seen in these parts — rare enough to keep Jane Jones giggling at the idea of it all the way through their polka. Giggling, and prodding him to see if he's real. Pulling his beard.

When she brought him his ham and eggs this morning he'd asked how old she was and given her his revolvers to look at.

'Sixteen,' she said, sighting along a Colt. 'Although couldn't I pass for eighteen at least?'

'Still a boy myself under the whiskers,' he said. Dancing just now, the curious springiness of her young sapling back bending against his hand.

'What a sweet touch, stealing a circus!' she said. Well, it was. What an extra treat for the prisoners, something to tell their grandchildren in the next century! How he'd turned on a circus for them as well as free drink and games of cards and the hop, step and jump competition (which he, sportingly handicapped by his holstered Colts — and fatigued by a night's hard riding — had allowed Jack McManus, the blacksmith's offsider, to win by eighteen inches), and his genial demonstration of crack shooting and, above all, now, the dancing to the concertina against the joyful flames of the bonfire.

Not that the circus owner hadn't been surprised and reluctant to be bailed up with sleep still in his eyes on a Sunday morning in his caravan on the Benalla Road.

'You bloody mad bushman! I'll set my lion on you!'

He just laughed. He couldn't take seriously a sleep-ruffled codger with a red-arsed monkey on his shoulder. The Great Orlando!

'Look sharp, or I'll tickle you up with this.' He pointed one of the revolvers. Mirth was already skittish from the lion and the monkey and rank things glaring from cages, but even with no sleep he'd felt relaxed and resolved back then at eight o'clock with the dawn's dew still laying the dust and his plans smoothly unfolding. One, Aaron just shot dead, as arranged. Two, the Police Special from Benalla therefore coming for them, as arranged. Three, the line torn up to send the train to hell, as arranged. Four, the Benalla banks thus unprotected, as arranged. Five, the townspeople all rounded up in the Glenrowan Inn, with drinks on them, as arranged. And they had a few more little arrangements up their sleeves. No wonder the monkey shot him spiteful looks; the circus was a bonus. When Mirth shied and snorted he reined her into a pirouette worthy of the ring.

'You should sign me up,' he told the circus owner. 'I'm Ned Kelly.'

Why did they always draw him as a maniac? All glaring eyebrows, matted hair and putrid bird's-nest beard. Lunatic's eyes and mouth like a bayonet slash. A nine-foot cannibal who'd slipped the chain from some madhouse or freakshow.

That picture showing him as a leering ogre straddling the Murray River! One widow-crunching boot set in Victoria, the other in New South Wales. Disembowelled police strewn about. Children's corpses trickling from his lips. Hangdog weeping women. After that one, he wrote an angry letter to the editor. MONSTER REPLIES! the rag screamed. Was there no justice in the press? Well, this time the *Melbourne Punch*, the *Australasian Sketcher* and the *Illustrated News* would have had to send their best artists, their top men.

This time they'd see something.

They'd also see what dapper was. This hacking jacket, these new tweeds. Kids squabbling to shine his boots. The beard now trimmed a stylish spade, this scarlet cravat blossoming out from under it. *And later in tonight's proceedings won't I be wearing the sash of honour, the green and gold!*

Their very own dashing devil would gleam like a nugget and smell like boronia.

Oh, yes, he'd been keeping track of the press's insults these last twenty months, been looking forward to making their personal acquaintance. The chamois leather gold-dust pouch from the Euroa bank was jammed with newspaper cuttings.

Devil incarnate of the Antipodes, Satan's right hand, our Mephisto, the Vulture of the Wombat Ranges, beast of prey, outback monster, rural sadist, flash young ghoul, savage yokel, bog-Irish fiend, homicidal maniac, corpse robber, cheap assassin, man of blood, bog butcher, jumped-up bush butcher, brute creation, crawling beast, jungle gorilla, creeping thing, reptile, viper in society's bosom, sewer scum, vermin, bog worm, peat maggot, maggot on a dead kangaroo, slippery goanna, dirty lizard, dingo, wild dog ('should be shot like a . . .'), snivelling cur, mad dog, dirty dog, pariah dog, cunning fox, pack wolf, shark, spineless jellyfish, strutting rooster, scrub bull, bush bully, cut-and-dried villain, hangman's customer, agrarian outcast and social bandit (these by 'An Educational Correspondent'), cut-rate highwayman, champion of the lower orders and street-corner loungers, evil marauder, predator, common thief, desperado, thug, ruffian, bad egg (ho-hum) —

— Things he'd been called by the gentleman of the press, *ta rah!*

A corner of the faintest memory flickered.

Hadn't Dad called him Sunshine?

So here at the inn, waiting for the Police Special, raring to go, is the so-called Kelly Gang:

Me, Edward Kelly, twenty-four.

Over there sipping brandy and trying his best to grow a moustache, my young brother Dan, seventeen.

Making eyes at Ann Jones, the landlady, loverboy Joe Byrne, twenty-one.

That jockey-shaped customer relaxing on the ottoman, bristling with revolvers and grizzling about his swollen feet, Steve Hart, nineteen.

All Irish boys and selectors' sons just happening to be in the same place at the same time — Stringybark Creek. Killed three police there before they killed us. Robbed banks, captured towns, lived in caves, drank pubs dry, stuck by each other, killed a traitor. Had war declared on us by Victoria, by New South Wales, by the Crown, by the Melbourne Club, by the London *Times*. The Queen in England proclaimed things against us; said anyone in the world is allowed to kill us. She strongly advocated it.

I guess that makes us a gang.

AND WAITING with them in the pub these last twenty-four hours are their sixty-two prisoners — waiting on them, pouring them drinks, serving them Sunday roast lamb and mint sauce, napping in corners, flirting with them, singing to them, toasting them, laughing with them, badgering them for dances and autographs and yarns of their adventures, sniggering at Dan's pack of saucy playing cards, bathing Steve's feet, doing what they ask. And the few here not their friends — Curnow, the schoolteacher; Stanistreet, the stationmaster; Bracken, the local constable — admire their manners and do it anyway. Well, maybe not Bracken. So he admires their weaponry and sits quiet.

And they are hospitable, amiable, insistent hosts.

Dance faster, Mr Curnow, in your soft schoolteacher's boots. Cheer up, Mr Stanistreet, what's a torn-up rail on a steep culvert, one train more or less? Drink up, Mr Bracken. Whoever heard of such well-mannered, responsible outlaws?

Now, for your entertainment and pleasure, ladies and gentlemen, the Kelly Gang brings you the famed acrobat and juggler, the Great Orlando! Watch him toss and catch those four whisky bottles he's helped empty!

This rowdy crowd is anxious to curry favour and restless in the policeman's vicinity. Dan and Steve, even Joe, are uneasy too. They want to keep Bracken handcuffed. But he, the leader, is feeling magnanimous. He winks as he tops up Bracken's glass.

'In case you're wondering,' he shouts to Bracken over the din of the concertina and the tipsy voices roaring the Kelly Song, 'I've confiscated the fancy throwing knives and the key to the lion's cage.'

The signal rocket from Dray's Peak arcs into the sky, rises with the lion's swelling roar and slowly flares across the membranes of his vision.

So the Peak contingent is in place and quietly waiting, too. Everything can begin. He wishes it could start now while he is still alert and optimistic, making his rounds like a general, moving back and forth from the verandah to the bright ruckus of the bar and the parlour and to the bonfire outside. And to the dark patch of bush behind the pub.

He sips from the eagerly proffered drinks, he listens (for a panicky train whistle, for the shrieking scrape of brakes, for a crash), he chats, he shakes hands, he slaps shoulders, he ruffles children's hair, he snatches moments to sit and think things through.

And every fifteen or twenty minutes he treads a path through the winter weeds to the same broad twisted gumtree trunk, its crown charred and hollowed into a turret by some ancient bushfire, and in the shadows behind it, in the clay around its roots, he urinates.

The image of the flare fizzes on his nerve impulses long after its smoky trail has drifted off and the tapering growl is just a shiver on the air and his exposed skin.

All the time lately these dreams he's younger and back with old Harry Power sticking up a Cobb & Co. on the Sydney Road. So real the dust dries into bogeys in his nose, the sun drums on his shoulders, the horse twitches and swells under him. An old coarse-maned strawberry roan.

The strange thing is, this coach turns and chases him. Off roads, across deep streams, up loose gravelly slopes, defying terrain and gravity. And it's packed with fuzzy pock-marked marksmen, turbaned troopers, fierce crack-heeled renegades in scraps of uniform ripped from mutilated white men, all smirking and firing weapons from the coach. Others, heroes' stolen medals stuck everywhere (on their crotches! in their hair!), spitting purple phlegm through filed teeth, encircle him with some lost regiment's artillery, and from high up every gumtree a grinning sniper snipes. All air around his head crisscrosses hot with bullets. Creasing his cheeks, his chin, his scalp. Oh, there's one through the tongue! The ear!

Wouldn't be so bad if he wasn't up to his stirrups in mud, if his gelding wasn't galloping backwards to the enemy, if this Martini-Henry hadn't turned into a droopy oxtail in his hand.

In real, waking life there's this certainty of who's coming after them this very minute, who'll try to kill them when he gets there — in five minutes, or thirty, or one hour, or six — who has no choice now. He more than knows this fact; he's counting on it.

Hare. Hare's in as deep as he is now. This is his affair too. Hare's with him and after him for the duration. For as long as it takes.

Hare's coming and he's waiting. They're all waiting with their new rapid-fire Winchesters, their shotguns and revolvers, their kegs of gunpowder, their maps and schemes and friends, their rested horses, their body armour. All these tricks up their sleeves. Just thinking about the train arriving and Hare's face when he sees them makes him grin and shiver at once. Does Hare also feel that twinge in the groin? That niggling, always-needing-to-piss sting?

AND HARE'S special Queensland blacktrackers have to be coming too, those barefoot bush shadows with their osprey eyes. This whole train crash is for their benefit! And also for his special Victorian troopers, the pride of Melbourne's lowest brothels and the shady side of Collins Street. And not forgetting those adventurous special correspondents, the gentlemen of the press, *ta rah!*

He likes to think of Hare jolted from his after-dinner cognac and Havana in the smoking room of the Commercial Hotel, Benalla, by the telegraph message that his special informer, Aaron Sherritt, had been most specially murdered. Fop and spy, apple of each other's eye. If Aaron's corpse doesn't bring Hare running, nothing will. Hare is shocked. Hare is disturbed. Yes, Hare is also raring to go.

So, you special squeaky-voiced Superintendent, not long now.

He'd swear you could almost smell Hare's anxious cigars, hear those praying-mantis limbs propping and pacing. Oh, that dampness on the forehead, that lank moustache and undertaker's pallor will never do for the Queen's languid hero.

And if by chance Hare lived, what a lovely hostage he would make. Easily worth an outlaw's mother.

In answer to that handsome black-haired lady in the corner . . . Madam, in this world and the next, these are the ones I hate:

I hate Constable Thomas Lonigan, shot clean through the temple, dead but not forgiven.

Senior Constable Hall, yes, that fat, gutless pistol-whipper and sly bribe-taker.

Constable Flood, horse-thieving bastard and hypocrite.

And that trooper's farthermost orifice, Constable Alexander Fitzpatrick, drinker of brandy-and-lemonade, dirty fighter, lying bully of women and children, poisoner of my name, corrupter of the law, perjurer before God. Even the Victorian police force has kicked him out. What more can I say? If he weren't such a spunkless rabbit I'd call him my worst enemy for starting all this.

Oh, and Judge Barry, Judge Barry, Judge Barry.

Not Hare, oh no. He will be my prize, my joy, our saviour.

SO WHERE did that leave Aaron? Charming, smooth-haired, smooth-voiced Aaron Sherritt, Australia's friendliest man, shot through his easy-going heart and brain just last night?

Somehow he couldn't hate Aaron. What he had felt was stronger and more bitter, but that was when Aaron was still alive. Today, right now, he was almost indifferent. Aaron was as much a part of this place as he was. He was just the other side, the side he'd never understand. The constantly obliging side. Every man's mate, every young girl's lover. The cool, dead, agreeable moon.

AND CURSE me for thinking just then: my father, Red Kelly. Not saying it but thinking it. Put him on the list for weakness, for having no stomach for prison, for puffing up like a snowman in passive protest, for languishing, squelching, on his bed. For dying of dropsy, an old man at forty-seven.

Laying him out in our hut at Avenel, she and I left imprints every spot we touched. Rolled him over and corked him up to stop him seeping, like a five-day drowned man.

No Requiem for my soggy father.

Oh, mother, truly his name just burst into my head like a blast of duckshot. I'm only eleven and a half. Oh Jesus forgive me.

AARON WOULD play a roo-gut banjo fretted with slivers of box-tree and overlaid with possum parchment. While he twanged, he sang a song about me that Joe dreamed up, them both harmonising, Joe thrumming on his bush bass made from a tea-chest and a broom-stick strung with twine.

Aaron sang a sweet, wild song about me in the

cold nights and still we killed him. In the firelight we'd do the polka to it to keep warm. A shotgun blast in the head, another in the chest. His pregnant wife, fifteen, wailing and kissing his mashed innards. Praying his forehead back to smoothly normal, unhappening the brain-bits on her stroking hands, the red spray patterning the air, the wall, the door jamb and fanning out like a lyrebird's tail. Well, he was a treacherous young banjo player. When in the mood he'd dance with stones in his boots – didn't mind, no coat or scarf, kicking up the frosty grass like a dervish. Liked the girls young; I said to him about Mary Hegarty, she's only just thirteen! He said, so what, I'm not superstitious. Went to gaol once for concussing a passing Chinaman with a rock, and for mistreating a horse. A treacherous banjo player and a heedless dancer.

Knew how to make you laugh, though, if you were in the mood.

Massacre, there's a word. Worse than killing, worse than murder, worse than slaughter. Massacre's what they said we did. *What I, the monster, did.* 'The Massacre at Stringybark Creek.'

But is it a massacre if they're shot going for their guns? If they're police? Just because the police aren't as good as us doesn't make it massacre. Anyway, massacre sounds like killing many more than three. (Maybe ten and over.) Massacre sounds like butchering the innocents. Massacre has the soft, crispy-moist, knife-blade sound, the stabbing, hacking, ruptured-vein sound. Massacre sounds like Indians slashing and scalping in the night. Massacre sounds like dead women and children, not armed troopers. Massacre surely doesn't sound like four men against four men. Massacre sounds like you relish flesh explosions and mutilations. *The sort of thing a maniac does.*

Can it be a massacre if you let one go? The only one who surrenders when ordered?

Would it be a massacre if the police had killed three of us instead?

Can it be a massacre if everyone's Irish?

Battle is the word I'd use for a fair fight. One side against the other.

Massacre . . . juicy word, though.

Was that the train or a rumbling and ringing in his ears? His imagination or thunder or just his hungry lion?

What this place needed was a watch-peacock. Better than any dog for warning when the police came by. No police spy much less a uniformed trooper ever snuck up on Eleven Mile Creek without their peacock giving the alarm. Simple city coppers just off the boat shat themselves at that sudden banshee scream from hell or somewhere very like it in the spooky outback dark.

He must keep thinking ahead, anticipating Hare and his ploys. There was no end to Hare's brainstorms, the best so far being his setting up policemen as horse thieves to try to tempt the gang's old business streak (as if the police didn't have proper horse thieves like Flood in their ranks anyway!) and dispatching that group of pretty horsewomen as police spies – this complex entrapment fancy of course going badly wrong, or badly right, depending on your view. (The Royal Melbourne Show dressage champion so impressed with Joe's *piaffe* that she strutted with him into the billiard room of the Royal Mail Hotel and stretched out on the baize might be of two minds on this.)

But the plan that took the cake was sending along those Irish detectives disguised as priests who offered to hear this gang of Catholic boys' confessions. Presuming that by now their Mick killer-leader would surely be seeking absolution.

Not so.

Maybe some men weren't meant to be released from guilt or obligation. Maybe some couldn't bear the sacrament of penance for sins they saw as necessary. Or maybe there were one or two simply beyond acquittal or forgiveness. Just like the lion would never make a watchdog – not distinguishing between friend and enemy, human and animal, hating every thing. All the time roaring that urgent, meaty need.

Air!

Breathing the trees, the winter grass, the old, cold, quartzite breath of rocks. Northerly breeze in his moustache whisking away lion, monkey, camel, horses, smoke, music, whisky, laughter, hoofprints, youth, ancient familiar whiffs of ammonia, cartridges and pistol barrels, dying pleadings and bodily whimperings. Breeze dry as a magistrate's eye. Breeze maybe too thick to hear a train through! There was some winter plant here smelled like semen. The scent on the verandah was more a taste, like yeast and hops and salt, and there was another female smell like warm gunmetal and blood in the mouth. In the air, the sound of some invisible tinkling nightbird and the creak of frost-chilled wood and rock. Too cool for crickets but a mad frog somewhere nearby answered the concertina.

He can taste their secret in the northerly wind, yes. Her impossibility. No names.

Mrs C.

THIS IS how she introduces herself: 'Good afternoon, would you come and hold my horse's thing?'

The lady loves the chase, and is famous in the district for hunting on this dark bay stallion. She rides Lord Byron so hard over such long distances that sometimes he doesn't have time to piss. When she makes her request it's a Monday afternoon – I'm employed shaping foundation stones – and Lord Byron's been holding on since Saturday's hunt.

This time his bladder's paralysed from the strain. Looks to me like colic, only worse. Two stablehands are struggling to hold him. He's groaning and slick with sweat, sighing, kicking at his swollen belly, peering with a longing, uneasy expression at his flanks.

This lady pushes her brown hair from her eyes, rolls up her sleeve, oils her arm and plunges up into Lord Byron's sheath. He's well retracted from pain and nerves. She frowns. 'Got it,' she says, and, grunting, hauls it all out and drops it across my hands.

'Hold on,' she tells me.

And then the boys and I all need to hold on very hard. Lord Byron trembles and skitters and lurches us back and forth across the paddock because she's got this veterinarian's metal catheter, Jesus, it must be five feet long, pointed at the business end, and she oils it too, and grabs him, pushes it inside and forwards and threads it ever upwards.

A terrible shiver overcomes Lord Byron. Suddenly we're up to our shins, nearly floating in the downpour, and shivering almost as much as him.

'There,' says Mrs C. 'Watch your boots.'

A SHOUT breaks his trance. They're urgently calling him back inside. His heart spears into his gullet in anticipation of something. What? The worst news. But this spasm is only the shock of remembering something: he kills people.

Then how come his prisoners' faces smile at the killer like courtiers?

And the cause of this noisy crisis? Old Martin Cherry, the roustabout and axe-sharpener, wants to show him his black cockatoo! This bird is supposed to always say, to have never since it was an egg until this second refrained from saying, 'Bail up, you bastards, I'm Ned Kelly!' So Martin and his drunken mates allege. So now, as if he had nothing better to do, he finds himself sitting in the parlour's best arm-chair admiring a tattered old cockatoo and gracing it with a bishop's smile. And its wrinkled crocodile eyes glare sideways through him as if he were its worst enemy on earth.

It refuses to speak. 'Give it some brandy!' orders Ann Jones. Someone pushes a glass under the bird's head; it blinks at the fumes, pokes in a tentative grey tongue, raises its crest pugnaciously, lowers it again, glances away, still says nothing human.

Time is standing still. All around him crowd these blurry, nodding, eager-to-please faces. Grubby chil-dren, too: Dick and Emma Reardon's five kids. Waiting for the cockatoo's momentous declaration, he's nodding too and slipping back into his trance. Within seconds he's left the fuggy parlour and the cockatoo's audience for the company of Kennedy, Scanlon, even Lonigan, all of them attending their own Requiem Mass at St Patrick's Cathedral. The policemen sit Irish-cheeked and pomaded in the front pew alongside him as well as lying waxy-stiff in their coffins. Oh, the sweet incense and the serious spit and polish! Kennedy and Scanlon are solemn in their dress uniforms and new posthumous medals but that creature Lonigan leans across to him, eyes his crotch and winks.

'Ned! Ned!' Mrs Jones is beaming brandy fumes at him. 'Say hello to your namesake! Give him a walnut!'

Now Kennedy and Scanlon get to their feet at Stringybark Creek, dust off their pants, stretch, wipe scabs from their faces, click tongues for their horses, shake hands with him. Black cockatoos rise like shrieking stormclouds from the stringybarks as the policemen trot off cheerfully. 'That was a good one, Ned. You had us there, you old bastard,' etc. And with crisp manly salutes, canter off to their families.

Kee-ah, kee-ah. The loudest wailing cry he's ever heard. It's his namesake screaming.

'Thank you, Mrs Jones, make it a double.' He tosses down the brandy, blinks and laughs at something private. Jesus, he forgot. It couldn't be St Pat's. He's read in the Argus that Kennedy'd had Baptist rites.

What's this in his other hand? Walnut shells? Jesus Christ. 'Give me another, Mrs Jones. I'll have what the bird's having.'

Can't bear the guilt of her in Pentridge – knowing the hard bluestone damp, the cold carbolic stink, her dark weevily loneliness.

At least the Yank can't get at her there. No passing trooper, drover, neighbour, hawker, miner, uncle, cousin, husband drunkenly chasing her, heaving his dinner at the wall, waving shotguns, horsewhips, cursing, threatening, burning the house down if she says no.

A notorious mother, that's a thing.

That's my mother you're doing that to.

The American twenty years younger than her presses his body against hers. Bumps her right there in front of us. Look away, look out the door, look back, he's still doing it, pressing. She's not moving. Her hand on his arm nonchalantly stroking hairs has blood around the nails from gutting rabbits. She won't look at any of us.

A string of entrails slithers to the floor and Dan's dog leaps in one fast slurp and gulp.

On sullen nights I start awake. The squeaking bed, the oaths and grunts, the shock of a stranger's vowels, and whining kids amid the slops, the slaps, the creaks and free-for-all — all overhung with waves of rum — and now someone's pissing in the pot. Romance.

You're my mother he's doing that to.

Keep the gutting knife under your pillow. Do it!

Ladies and gentlemen — thank you, thank you — I've been asked to relate how I got started in my outlaw ways. Young John Jones over there asked me that very question; only a boy, so you can't blame him for his ignorance. Johnny, keep out of the sherry and listen. You might learn something.

Well, they locked up my mother, didn't they?

Police's version has me evil from the start, born into a bad-blooded family on both sides, to be stamped out like rabbits, like some sort of plague. They tut-tut about my riding with Harry Power the bushranger at fourteen and holding up the squatter McBean. And the fight with the Chinaman named Ah — pardon me, ladies — Fook. Couldn't make those charges stick but they went on my record just the same.

But, don't laugh, it was a pair of calf's — excuse me again — testicles that first landed me in gaol. Got me six months in Beechworth, truly.

This summer day I'm with Ben Gould and my uncle castrating calves when Gould suddenly wraps up one prize set in a quickly scrawled note which says *Try these instead*. He just tells me, 'Here, give these to that old woman Jeremiah McCormack.'

Everyone's in that odd, sour mood that castrating brings on. Also a bit edgy in the heat, and blood-speckled. I'm still fourteen, feeling my oats, more muscle than brains then. There'd been some disagreement earlier over us borrowing one of McCormack's horses. Well, I ride up and hand over the parcel. And I'm so dozy *I stick around*. McCormack starts spitting chips, says he can welt me or any of my breed. Throws the balls splashing in my face. I'm jumping off to accept the challenge when his wife whacks my horse in the flank with an ox bone. The horse jumps forward and my fist comes into collision with McCormack's nose and causes him to lose his equilibrium.

I didn't twig the real thing that Gould was needling him about, that the McCormacks were childless, that McCormack couldn't do his marital duty. Wonder how many of these other scars and cranium dents I owe to raucous misunderstandings and blissful ignorance.

No, really, it's no joke. Disorderly conduct, plus obscene behaviour. A serious affair. It brought me to the attention of that avid reader of the *Police Gazette*, Senior Constable Hall. You know how the *Gazette* summed me up? 'Subject to riding horses.' How's that for an epitaph?

Thank you, thank you.

ROBBING THE first bank is like the silkiest good dream. Hovering above myself, watching me doing it, hearing this half-stranger's sharp voice ring out. Me but not me inside, here *and* there but not entirely there or here. There I am pointing the bloody gun and giving the orders. Here I am looking into the worst fears realised in those clerkish eyes.

There I am – *hello!* – suddenly the man in charge of Death and Money.

Naturally, the real pleasure's in the handing over of

the cash. There's no neater transaction – I love it. They hand all their money to me; I take all their money from them. *Hmm. Would they jump to it quite so briskly if I weren't the country's most famous killer?* And the dream is suddenly complete. Nothing goes sour, like in a real sleeping dream. No disappointing tricks – the money doesn't turn to air or turds or feathers in my hand. I take the lot. I heft the bags. Yep, the cash is absolutely *there.* Take a look: the notes are stacked; the coins are heavy, round and perfect; no missing chunks, no blue uniform (no Fitzpatrick!) looming in the corner to blast my hopes. New notes, soft chamois bags of gold dust. And I don't say no to worn notes either, good assay samples, title deeds, promissory notes, mortgages, anything sealed or signed or stamped with Her Majesty's porky profile; it's all bank business, embossed by the other side, rich people's stratagems.

So – make a bonfire of the ledgers and the poor men's debts and canter off with the rest, these swollen bags of luck. I took a risk. Let the grapevine spread the word: yes, I've pulled off this coup. And the other boys weren't bad either.

Feels right for once. Officer in charge of retribution, the official bogeyman. Bursting from my cave, storming down from the grim and barren ranges, throwing lightning bolts – *Woo-woo!* – through the rainbow and onto the sunny plains. I'm the wearer of the green and gold and no complaints. No more chasing the centaur's shadow. I'm it. *I am it.* Oh, Jesus, banks are fun.

The papers said Joe and Dan and Steve and me were always a gang but that's not true. We got stuck with each other at the killings and had to quickly get organised.

Before then Aaron was a friend. I was really closer to my next brother Jim than to young Dan. The gang could easily have had Aaron, Jim, my cousin Tom Lloyd Junior and Wild Wright as well. They just weren't there at that moment. Jim was shearing in the Riverina, Tom was scouting the police for us a mile north. Aaron, well . . .

We were all selectors' kids growing up around the town of Greta. We were just acquaintances – the Greta Mob. Once we'd made a name we were promoted by the police and papers to Gang. But kindred spirits was all we were — mostly Catholic boys and girls and brothers-in-law and people's sisters and mothers and grandads. Everyone bar the police, the squatters and the Chinese diggers. They were all their own gangs. You can't tell me the police aren't a gang! The squatters!

First awake some mornings, I gaze at the ruffled, sleeping heads of — so the Age *and* Argus *reckon — the country's, the Empire's, greatest scourge. That mouth-breather Dan, dribbling in his sleep, looks thirteen or less, and his downy cheek when he wakes — from lying on his saddlebag — stays tattooed with his pillow's stitching well into the afternoon. Steve, fluffier-faced, a few orange bristles on his chin, snores softly with one eye eerily half open, a wary cub, a jacket of his father's wound around him as a comfort. Soon these two'll be cackling around the fire, elbowing each other, punching arms, pinching food, preparing for another day of continuous eating, whistling, spitting, smoking, competing with their guns and farts and dicks — and occasionally, suddenly, remembering to be serious and responsible outlaws.*

In their overheated way it was the papers that defined us, presented us as sure things, as blocks of type. And when they declare you to be so-and-so, then you become it. Strange the way they make you famous or notorious before you are – and then you are in spades.

Until the killings, even Dan and me we weren't that organised. Weren't as smart as they claimed we were and then savagely attacked us for becoming. We took things as they came, drank and played the goat too much. But I guess we four were always flash. The best riders and shooters ended up together. And we had the steel of grudge; we were the Micks who hit back twice as hard. I guess we chose ourselves, the ones with umbrage. And we did get smart, didn't we?

We chose Aaron too. Make no mistake, he was good at it, seemed well worth choosing. Maybe even worth the second chance we gave him. Rode well, fought well and told a better joke than me. Had more looks and charm than all of us, except maybe for Joe.

A peculiar thing about Aaron: he never wore a coat. He showed off by sleeping outdoors in his shirtsleeves in midwinter. He'd stretch out anywhere like an old cattle dog – on a frosty rock, wet grass, a heap of gravel – and instantly nod off. And then he'd grin and talk, carry on conversations in other languages in his sleep. These strange sounds and smiles, this flickering going on all over his face.

Don't mind admitting it spooked me when he did that. I mean, we've all lived outdoors, in caves, put up with cold and suffering – but only to escape and survive, not to impress, not *on purpose*. I've been thinking there's a certain sort of black tribesman I've heard of that reminds me of Aaron. This person bends in the wind, blends into the background. Mostly he employs the help of the dead to destroy other people.

A night dancer, they call him.

BUT HARE was fascinated by that spartan stuff. Most impressed with his ruddy, handsome spy. His Aaron was officer material. Well, Aaron impressed some things on me too: that you're doomed without an aim, that the strong can still be spineless. You've got to choose a side. The trouble with Aaron was he didn't know how weak he was. Or even *who* he was. I think that's why he slept so light. In case he danced away from himself in the night.

But now he's sleeping like a top.

So, Mr Bracken, if you want outlaws, you couldn't organise it better. Locking up a mother of ten on perjured evidence is guaranteed to work. Molesting their sisters, raiding homes, frightening children. Your man Fitzpatrick managed all of this. And topped it off by whining that I shot him. (In the hand! And made him faint!) I wasn't even home.

Let me state the bloody obvious. A charge of attempting to murder a policeman has them after you then and forever.

If I *had* been there I wouldn't have shot him in the hand!

So Dan and me saddled up and took off to Bullock Creek. Joe Byrne was doing nothing so he came too. A bit later Steve Hart joined us. They couldn't catch us so they gave our mother three years' hard labour. Judge Barry did the sentencing, roaring from the bench that if he caught me he'd give me fifteen years. Judge *Sir* Redmond Barry, sorry, being knighted twice already by the Queen for his firm dealings with us ignorant bushmen. The lower orders and dangerous classes. In other words, the Irish.

We weren't a gang then, we were just the shrewdest of the ordinary, wily with those special things the Irish know. The never knowing when we'd had enough, the never leaving well enough alone.

Her breasts were nightly visions bending over me. Yes, I thought them up all round and brown and became something, someone, else again. I was still young is my excuse, but no excuse, got something from it anyway, from these ghostly sights and feels of her. Helped me through the days and nights and daily fights, her dark hair dripping on my face. Me nuzzling with bruised lips and cheeks.

This is difficult to even think of, in case I'm overheard. Wouldn't trust anyone not to read my mind. *Dad in heaven, ginger eyebrows glaring down!* Didn't even say this in confession, in the days I went.

Well, it shocked me once to hear this sucking sound, woke me with a fright, dry-mouthed, but it was only me.

Beechworth Gaol, 1869; just turned fifteen, this was.

I can hear it, that one question fizzing unvoiced in every timid mind: Did you, *ahem*, or did you not — as was announced, and pardon me for asking, never believed it myself, of course, of a man like you, such strangeness, *umm*, excuse me, but there being only one of them remaining on the sergeant's head — CUT OFF KENNEDY'S EAR?

Well, police, papers, Protestants say so, pray for, scheme of, this propaganda. The sadist stole his heirloom watch, tied him to a tree, tortured the man, sliced off his ear in some drunken Celtic rite. Revenge, maybe, on a Catholic turning Rechabite. The madman heard his wounded plea — The wife! The kids! — but shot him anyway.

That part's true. Of course I can't stand slow

bleeding deaths, blowflies, bull ants, stinging, nibbling things. I've put many a horse in better health out of its misery. Certainly I pushed the gun against his heart – sorry Sergeant, sorry, wish it wasn't you in this melodrama, many, many I'd prefer, and so forth – and pulled the trigger, pulled a cloak over him with care, left him honourably, the shot still roaring in both his ears.

The myth arose of us boys sharing blood guilt at Stringybark Creek, of promising to die as one if necessary. They said the four of us shot him in a pact to split the blame. Wrong. Compared me to a chieftain from the mists of Irish history who forced his men to ritualistically blood themselves by firing into corpses. Jesus, you'd think the police'd know about shotgun wounds, multiple entry. The swandrops blast was mine alone. I shot him – and the other two as well. Me. In too deep from the beginning. Deep and rooted as any tree an Englishman could name.

Something gnawed off his ear, is what I'm saying. Wombat, dingo, crow, fox – take your pick.

What do you think I am? A bloody monster?

BUT — AND something else. I kept his watch. Genuine Swiss movement, pretty fob chain, no sense it lying there in the weather. It wasn't just the watch alone: we took their guns and rations, horses, everything of use. Souveniring from the enemy happens in every war. Thought of sending it to his family but by then the papers had me down as ghoulish — the Ear Cutter, the Corpse Robber, shameful, not my usual style and so forth — so I thought, no point now, I'm damned anyway, a gold watch is a gold watch. Ran two minutes slow a day, as it happened. A bit later I gave it to a barmaid with a lovely Kerry blush who didn't mind my eyebrows.

'When you smile like that your mouth's not hard at all,' she said.

I said nice things back. Who wouldn't?

GLAD TO be rid of it, but the watch still niggles at me. A blot on my copybook, I know it. Dream of it, of giving it back, at least once a week. Dream of other round things too. Coins, cakes, necklets, plates, the rims of cups. Even globes of the world. But when I peer closer at these circles, there's always a chunk missing from them. I have this gold coin in my hand, a treasure. I'm thrilled. Then I see an eighth, a quarter's gone. And over my shoulder, Fitzpatrick's smirking.

A watch! It smacks of the common bushranger, the city pickpocket. The sort of petty job old Harry Power did. When I rob, I rob bloody towns!

Ransacked his pockets! Jesus, forgive me playing into their hands. I disgust me sometimes, getting in the way of my own aims.

'Dan, listen for the train. Water that brandy, for God's sake! Sharpen up!'

THE SIGHT of a corpse fosters the heebie-jeebies in any man who believes in the Last Judgement. And in anyone who doesn't.

So they say.

Should tell Curnow that creeks and me together didn't always signify death. That when I was aged eleven back home at Avenel I was the Hero of Hughes Creek.

Coming home from school, that studious fat boy Richard Shelton slipped off the tree that bridged the deep reach of the creek. Already tightly dressed and sausagey, then sucking sudden muddy water and disappearing with his goody-goody satchel of books around his neck. Jumped in after him, in the darkest part – the reddy-brown part when you open your eyes – the water rushing cold, snags plucking at me, imagining yabbies nipping tasty dead Richard in some clay-hole. Found him with my feet, pulled his bag off him and dragged him to the bank, squeezed him till he coughed up mud and cried for mum.

The Sheltons kept the general store and butcher's shop opposite the Royal Mail Hotel. Mr Shelton shook my hand, said a thank-you speech, gave me a green and gold sash for saving his son.

I wore it seriously, my hero's sash of green and gold. See, I can say. Proof I've saved a life as well.

FIRST THE simultaneous shot and cry — a sort of choking croak and unbelieving scream — then the falling down, the moaning for the wife and kids as breath leaves with a hiss and whistle, the arcs of blood into the air (the spurting bleeding going on for quite a time), then the sudden, buzzing silence and congealing, the stiffening (blowflies well established, plus a curious ant or two), the drying out (crows flop over to investigate), the stretching, the discolouring (joined by ants in larger numbers), the swelling, the smelling, the oozing (maggots now pop out), the exploding (bush rats and other small nibbling animals appear), the vaporising (beetles join the crowd, a blue-tongue lizard comes by), the melting (worms). All covered in this pale blue and sea-green mould of the finest, densest waving filaments.

Then him sitting up suddenly and roaring, 'Which one of you parasites took my ear?'

This is Kennedy in one of his nightmares.

You'll have to speak up, Mr Curnow, I can't hear you over the lion. Can we talk about my motives? Perhaps an overreaction on my part? Oh, we're on a single track here, aren't we? You don't know the half of it. That's the trouble when your story's seen through other eyes.

When did things first enter a different dimension? Well, now, that's the thing.

Doesn't it roar! Nightmare stuff, Mr Curnow.

What do schoolteachers dream of instead of lions?

REMEMBERING MYSELF as a boy is hard enough. A little child with toys, on foot, a toddling baby, impossible.

Back home at Avenel, did I, a grubby bundle, ever ride on my father's shoulders, ever catch a ball, put on his hat for laughs, his big boots? I can't say.

Hold his hand? Ever touch his prickly cheek? I can barely think this — kiss him? Who knows?

I'm a bearded man on a horse. Seems as if I always was, always will be.

What I best recall is riding alone with the sun behind me from Eleven Mile Creek to Greta, and seeing my shadow cantering ahead against the roadside weeds and willows. Leaving me stretched far behind, galloping to chase it, it seemed like a centaur from the picture books.

Do I tell a lie?

Remember that red evening of my running to greet him at the door, my joyful gripping of his legs that smelled of horse. Remember the slanting sunrays in the doorway, the golden specks of dust, the ruckus of the kookaburras' dusk chorus. He'd had a drink and was ready for games with his first son. So I barrelled into him and — here's a trick! — stuck my head between his knees and began to crawl on through this daddy tunnel. And he laughed and squeezed the trap together tight and kept on squeezing. Squeezed too hard and long to be a joke. Pressured my head and ears with this serious wrestling hold until I heard and saw the last red gongs of sunset beating and cried his name.

Against his will he does it, recalls life at Avenel. Avenel's really just the Sydney Road, but you can take your pick of sights. Shelton's general store. The Avenel Arms and Royal Mail Hotel. The wine shanty, selling plonk from the Tabilk vineyards. The black-smith's. The courthouse behind the police barracks.

The cemetery.

Travelling north and south, the Overland Mail, the Cobb & Co. and Crawfords' stagecoaches, bullock wagons, squatters on their bloodstock, farmers' families driving gigs, Chinese in traps and pattering past on foot. Flickering around the edges, shy Aborigines. The lunatic cart from Beechworth madhouse grinds by; shorn and bulbous heads stare out and catch your eye; only a giggle somewhere breaks the spell. The gold coach from the diggings, its escort uniformed in dusty white and blue, sabres clattering in scabbards, striving to impress now they're safely in a town (and with the night to spend constructively), speeds up and thunders down the road, swings into the police yard and stops dead.

And a different show: the gaol coach from the goldfields, bound for Beechworth. A small crowd watches this one, grows silent as the thieves and murderers, shackles rattling, peer out ferociously, step down and turn into doddery old men, shuffle between their keepers, and enter the lockup for the night.

And more, yes, he remembers Dan Morgan's severed head passing slowly through the town when he was ten. People muttering at the open cart, not impressed. Pale Dad, their Red, disgusted, saying, 'Turn away.' Because he's already sick with the dropsy and maybe sensing he has only months to go himself, Dad doesn't look. But himself on tiptoes. What's in the box, a livid blue melting into purple, doesn't seem like a former human anyway, with the beard stripped off as well for a police tobacco pouch.

They said Melbourne University had claimed the

head to study what had ever possessed it to think of crime. Phrenologists longed to feel its bushranging bumps. Morgan's gift to science. But the wonder to him was why the police overseeing the head were laughing.

Bear with me.

And straight from this, it seems, the peacock's screaming. Police are banging on the door, searching the house, backhanding them, kicking the dog, scattering hens, dropping jugs and dishes, smashing eggs on the floor. (The local squatter has lost a calf! *Shit, eh.*) Taking Red for possession of a calfhide with no brand. Arrested for possessing something *absent*. (Not crazy at all. He's got a record, after all. Didn't unlawful possession of two pigs get him transported in the first place?) He's sick at heart his Irish past's come back to haunt him twenty-four years later. Sick, he goes to court to get a twenty-five pound fine, in default, six months' hard labour. (Guess who's the magistrate? The same calf-less squatter!) Sick, Red comes out of gaol to welcome Grace, child number eight. He stays sick.

Neighbours rally with a pine coffin, dig a grave, help hoist him in. Can't afford a headstone but he's got a view of the courthouse and gaol traffic, the display of passing loonies. It's given to his eldest son to fill out the death certificate: Wife Ellen 34, children Mary Jane (dec.), Ann 13, Edward 11, Margaret 9, James 7, Daniel 5, Catherine 4, Grace 1.

He dips the pen in the government ink again and corrects the register, adds a ½ to Edward. It's official – Edward is now a serious eleven *and a half*. Maybe he always was.

Once he was planing timber for someone's window frame and showed me how. Watching the shavings curling from this steady instrument, his calm elbow, the patient process, the smooth levelness of the result – in my concentration I nearly swooned.

Must have planed for all of ten or fifteen minutes this cool and magic day of to-and-fro. Paying me attention. The air was all enclosed and warm around the two of us. Sweet wood smell. In my daze he called me Sunshine.

Bear with me, folks, and imagine this yellow early-summer's day when I come out of gaol, not long fifteen.

You'll want some fun, says Wild Wright, the horsebreaker, lending me his favourite chestnut mare. Ride her into Wangaratta, jumping fences all the way. So joyful to be out, I cut a swathe and talk to girls outside the Star Hotel. *Like my horse? Want a ride?* The publican's daughters say yes and share their nougat. And watching them trot around the town, their thick hair-weight bouncing on their backs, their fronts — excuse me — bouncing nicely too, it seems that life ahead will be one long November Saturday of nougat and girls.

The mare is pretty, and well-known for her white

blaze and docked tail. Known in the *Police Gazette*, as it turns out, for belonging to the Mansfield postmaster. But this is news to me when Constable Hall comes up behind me and tries to pull me off her.

In the struggle he lands in the dust and the mare gallops away. I run to catch the horse and Hall tries to shoot me! Snaps four shots at me with his Colt — and misses. So I stop and stand the stillest of my life while he comes up, trembling, says I'm arrested, and cocks the gun again.

What can I do to stay alive but dummy, then jump at him, grab the gun with one hand and his collar with the other?

The problem is, do I hit him now? Pound him senseless, put in the boot? A little Beechworth stomp I learnt inside? Ha! I'm still on a bond from gaol, so if I hit him to save myself, I go back in — and my sureties lose their bond money. And if I don't, he shoots me!

So I trip him, throw him in the dirt, keep tripping and throwing him until we're across the street — about the spot where Mrs O'Brien's hotel stands now. There's a post-and-rail fence, and I throw the coward on it on his belly. I have to get his gun, so I straddle him and root both spurs into his thighs while he roars like a calf and shifts several yards of fence. And he's still gripping his gun like grim death.

All the while he's yelling and soon two black-smiths and five other gawpers jump in to help him. I still can't fight them back and break my bond. They get ropes and tie my hands and feet. Hall pistol-whips me so hard across the head that when my mother comes for me, she tracks us across the street and into the cells by my blood trail in the dust.

It's another yellow summer's day when I'm loaded in the cart for court, in irons, and roped to the seat for good measure. Three years' hard labour for felo-niously receiving a horse. Only eighteen months for Wright, who stole it, and for Hall a cash reward from the local squatters for putting us away.

No, Mr Curnow, I was never convicted of actual stealing, though thanks for asking. But I have a con-fession for you. I wholesaled and retailed more horses than anyone in Victoria — except for Constable Flood. Flood used to claim all the stray horses listed in the

Police Gazette. Sold most of them to the navvies on the railway line. One bay cob he stole and sold four times before the line was finished. Meanwhile he was gaoling selectors' children just for petting squatters' ponies. Arrested Dan aged five or six for riding one. Locked him up. Locked up my mother for complaining. Even the magistrate, a squatter himself, laughed that one out of court.

Ho-hum. Next question.

He shakes his head, tut-tuts in understanding. But his eyes, the set of his mouth, say otherwise. He thinks my reasons for embarking on this campaign are trivial.

Bloody schoolteachers.

Sour, spermy smells of gaol again and this time rotting seaweed too. This time, in irons, he's in a road gang in the May Day Hills, then Pentridge, then a prison hulk, the *Sacramento*, anchored in Hobson's Bay off Point Gellibrand. There goes his youth into the official particulars: *Height 5 feet 10 inches, weight 11 stone 4 pounds, sallow complexion, hazel eyes, dark brown hair, broad visage, low forehead, eyebrows meeting, first growth of a beard, age 15 years 9 months.*

Nine scars listed on his face, running north to south.

Sallow complexion! Low forehead! Eyebrows meeting! Strong evidence of his criminal nature, if not membership of the apes!

Those old fishy prison lags not put off by scars and fierce eyebrows give the boy a try. He can state that none of them succeeds. (Every prisoner claims that, but convicts can pick the truth. Something missing in the eyes thereafter gives it away, they say; the spark goes out.) Most of them he just glares at and says nothing. Those toadfish that keep trying, or gang up on him, he warns he'll kill.

'All day,' he says, 'I'm handling picks and bars and sledgehammers, and handy with them.' He's in a work party of trustees quarrying bluestone and building piers around the bay. 'You won't always be together,' he says. 'You'll need to sleep sometime, and without dreaming of a crowbar through the skull.'

These gaol dregs are so dense you've got to get it across that you're quite prepared to die yourself before they take the message in, before they understand the fact of that calm and tight-closed fury and give up.

But one afternoon behind the Newport breakwater, one lag's so crazed he won't. He pulls out two ugly things, one a gaol-made knife, grins another sickly grin and makes another stab. The boy just shrugs and quickly moves. In fact, he doesn't need a pick or hammer with all the man's got on his mind. He takes one cut on the elbow, whips a spiky branch of kelp across the straining face and the lag trips on his own dropped pants and without fuss has his jewels stamped in the sand.

When he comes off the hulk he's just eighteen, six foot, with a beard. Double the scars. A quieter man who hates the smell and sight and motion of the sea. At least now he can imagine hell: a greasy winter shore bisected by a loamy rivermouth, a city's slimy bay, froth-stained with tar and sawdust, phlegmy flotsam, puffy things with pecked-out eyes. And on the high-tide line, strings of smelly sea-grapes pretending to be rosaries.

Well, why not? He's seen the sea as gaoler, molester, killer — and graveyard, too, for countless bloated cats and dogs, several cows, two drunkenly shotgunned sea lions, one pig and three people, one a street-girl still in her stays but minus her head. He's jumped aside as four spooked Clydesdales bolted a dray of pitch and bluestone foundations off the end of the Gellibrand pier like it was a cartload of feathers. And seen them every day for a fortnight after, in frozen frenzied gallop down below, still in harness, crabs and toadfish politely diminishing them from the lips and nostrils backwards. Until a pack of tiger sharks with a taste for everything but the stone and iron wheel-trims cancelled the tableau in twenty minutes.

He'd face the gallows before doing it again.

She's got a shock for me, she says, as I walk in the door. She's marrying George.

George?

The baker. The American.

Well, she's right. I'm shocked. Coyly asks me to be a witness. Everything's so wrong, I squirm. I've just got out of gaol. Can't I sit down first, have a drink, take my boots off? She's a flickery version of herself, she's lost her grip. She mixes frowns and giggles and holds up bolts of cloth for me to nod at. A wedding gown! She skids around the house, not finishing jobs, ignoring children, dabbing at her hair like she's eighteen, not a widow.

George can get the cake for free!

He doesn't much fancy the Pope, the groom

announces, if it's all the same to her, so they do the deed in Benalla according to the rites of the Primitive Methodists. Well, who's ever heard of them?

Of course he doesn't last the distance. Soon rides smiling down one Sunday morning to the hawker's wagon for a new axe-head and forgets to bring it home, or himself with it. Children numbers nine and ten are his. George M. King was his full name, not the best advertisement for California, Protestants or the baking trade.

He hasn't been as bone-and-muscle tired as this since she married King. For a month after the wedding he'd just kept drinking rum, more or less forgotten to eat, then woke one morning with a violent craving for the Diggers' Special at the Bellevue Tearooms in Beechworth. The Pork De Luxe With Eggs. This feast was a legend in the district. Streaky bacon, fried pork steaks, smoked shoulder ham, a slab of brawn, a bottom stratum of boiled trotters, all neatly layered in a mound, grouted with navy beans and crested with four fried eggs so that the pierced yolks flowed down the hill.

He ate the lot before the eggs had dried into a trickle, stirred three sugars into his milky tea, barely made the street outside. Great rattling, gripping gurgles shook his bowels. Only nineteen and shitting sheets of water like an old cow in a lupin field.

In that month, spaces where his memory used to be were filled with sentimental confidences and pointless arguments, surprised strangers' busted noses. Sometimes after blurry midnight flurries with seasoned barmaids by the Broken River, he woke alone with blistered eyelids to frightening crow calls in the high sun-glare and thought himself pecked blind and hollow.

That month he had to keep one eye closed to focus on what and whom he was doing. One eye closed against the savage sunshine, the scathing peacock, on the rare times he rode home.

Something had to happen, better or much worse. Maybe a tiger snake bite while sleeping out. A final drunken roll down the riverbank. Who'd have thought him lucky to be arrested for riding (while passed out) across a footpath? There were burrs in his hair, grass and piss stains on his pants when they took him in a cart, unconscious, over the Broken River to the Benalla police station. Here a Sergeant Whelan, who remembered him from other matters, was in charge. Whelan took three troopers, Constables

Lonigan, Fitzpatrick and O'Dea, along next morning to escort him — now on his feet, just — across the road to court.

As if four men weren't safeguard enough for one hungover youth, Fitzpatrick decided to handcuff him too. At this the prisoner stirred, swore loudly and lashed out. Fitzpatrick grabbed him by the throat and Lonigan the scrotum. Lonigan held on and on, and in this way they dragged him across the street and into the court.

By this time he was sharp with pain and fury, snapped out of crapulence. His drink was hocussed, he insisted to the magistrates, to get him back in gaol. He was loud, alert, persuasive, and, surprisingly, let off with a fine.

But he wasn't finished. On the courthouse steps he yelled a threat. Said he'd never shot a man yet but if he did, so help him God, Lonigan would be the first.

Did you hear that down the back? The lady said what a pity, *ahem*, such a strapping young fellow should have become an outlaw and did I ever consider going straight?

Madam, I must say it's not as cut and dried as that. Things flow over into other things. You don't wake up one morning saying, I've seen the light, today I'll toe the line, be the coppers' boy. But you could say that in the mid-seventies I had two years of intense law abiding.

I worked as a timber feller for Saunders and Rule, cutting sleepers for the Wangaratta–Beechworth railway, then for another sawmiller, Heach and Dockendorf, in the Mansfield district, then back to S. and R. as sawmill overseer at Bourke's Waterhole.

When the sleeper contract ran out I went prospecting up the headwaters of the King River and found commercial gold on Bullock Creek. Then cut and shaped thirty cartloads of quarry stone – using my Point Gellibrand experience – for a squatter's homestead.

Also had some honest paid fun, you'll be pleased to hear, trick-riding around the country shows and boxing for fair purses. You're speaking to the unbeaten heavyweight boxing champion of north-eastern Victoria.

Thank you, thank you, very kind.

I CAN bend from the saddle at full gallop and snatch a lady's handkerchief from the ground. I can stand and lie on the saddle at full gallop. I can jump fences kneeling on the horse's back.

Beat Wild Wright in the yard of the Imperial Hotel, Beechworth, in 1874. Twenty rounds, bare-knuckle. Officially organised – timekeeper, seconds, referee. Wright six-one and fourteen stone, me one inch and two stone less. Knocked him out in the twentieth. Anyone can look it up. Teach him to lend me that postmaster's mare.

Some women, not the youngest ones, like such shows. Like to see a strong younger man wounded but prevail, bending easily to snatch their handkerchiefs.

She packed a generous wicker basket; she'd been on many picnics. She laid a woollen rug on layers of pine needles and angled between two pine trees so the sun divided it. Explained that this way we'd be both warm and cool. Then she smoothed it, laying finger-nails lightly on my wrist, my upper arm, in passing. Like a lorikeet's claws, soft but serious. You knew they rested there only momentarily and could scratch if they wanted, but were grateful for the favour. She pecked at this, nibbled at that, peered at me intently from time to time with her face half slanting away to look at me better, like a brilliant rare bird on a stump.

'All that cutting stone and so forth, no wonder you're so hungry,' she said. 'Won't it be a lovely house?'

I've always liked the sighing sound air makes in a

pine tree, like wild women's whispers. One side of her mouth turned up, the other down. A small mole above it got pursed up when she hummed opera.

'Indeed,' I said, unable now to imagine her ever indoors. I gulped down every foodstuff, couldn't stop from eating.

Shapely lips started things. Then I did.

She dismissed the picnic with a wave. She brushed aside the bread and gammon and satsuma-plum jam, the sliced muskmelon, the lemon barley water, and lay back on the rug. The crickets paused, the breeze dropped dead. Never seen such sights in daylight. Never seen such keen foam down there before, and the colour on her cheeks and neck went pink, then scarlet, like those inland salt-lake parrots they sell in town. Lost in herself like younger women never are – a little pressure here, just there, oh, yes. Isn't that a funny place to feel such sensations, the artery running smoothly into there, pumping like a honeyeater's heart.

Little grass-ticks scurried up my legs and burrowed in my thighs and I let them. Sunshine on her alabaster belly and her birdcalls.

JESUS, PICNICKING gives you an appetite. Buttering another crunchy bun and munching fast – crumbs exploding from my lips – I say, 'It's probably not the time to mention that I once took a thoroughbred or two of his. For his own good your husband ought to change his brand. I didn't even need to burn it out and brand them again.'

Explained how easily I plucked the hairs and pricked the skin with iodine, made the C into a perfect Q for Quinn, my mother's maiden name – and my rowdy relatives'. 'Now they're cantering happily in New South Wales. The horses, I mean.'

She frowned, then rolled her eyes and laughed. Her little finger traced our silvery snail-trails on her thigh. She dabbed me carefully dry with her silky petticoat, pushed it deep into her face, caressed her nose and cheeks, inhaled the silk, then slowly unrolled it, shook the creases out and put it on. This side of her was newly strange again. Her eyes and smile while doing this were coming from some humid foreign place. The crickets by now were used to us and started up again their hot vibration. A whiff of hot gunmetal came off her, or maybe me. I felt like someone living another way of life so thought I'd better act like it. Pressed on her trigger again just where she said to and watched her colours change. Already longing for those birdcalls – the seagull, the parrot, the magpie carolling at the sun. Then pulled her back down on me and let her falling hair shield my eyes against the glare.

This was in my law-abiding time, in the early stages with Mrs C.

In the final stage with Mrs C, I made an appearance on her croquet lawn, burnt naked and caked in blood. Sizzled flakes of flesh and cloth flew off us all, spikes of our clotted hair snapped off. None of us was normal. Dan, tied on behind me, was making hooting noises in the wind.

All through those days of thirsty hiding, of guzzling blood and lurching in fires, I'd pictured her juicy green lawn. So the four of us, doubling up on two charred and limping horses, waving shaky guns, appeared like a mad nun's nightmare in the home paddock of Mrs C.

This was a week or so after Hare's men poisoned our dam with three strychnine-baited pigs and a decomposed roo or two, then set alight our hideout country to flush us out. A hot February drought, with the bracken and wattle undergrowth drier than touchpaper and all the streams lower than mud. Fires surged along the gullies and up across the ridge in separate bright gashes like cutlass wounds. As the main fire came up on us on the nor'westerly we fled our hut with a neck-bag each of dubious water and the four relief horses carrying hasty packs. Panic flowed in waves from horse to smoking horse and back. In the smoke and noise, Dan's mare Erina stumbled and Dan led her on foot in giddy spirals until we found them half-buried in the silt of what had been Six Fingers Creek sucking river stones and with their hair on fire from the ash of weeping-willow leaves.

Spewing in the saddle from bad water, shitting too, losing more moisture from our streaming eyes, we were scorched husks by the time we'd found a granite overhang to shelter under and let the main fire jump us. By the time I'd calmed Dan down from gibbering for mother and we'd kept ourselves alive a day, we'd drunk all the water anyway. The horses were colicky and mad from eating burnt feed but Erina was the maddest so while Dan was out to it again we cut her throat, not quite looking at each other, and drank the blood.

This way we lasted another two days. In daylight we hid under rocks from the police patrols, at night we doubled back behind them across the burning hills. Even the blacktrackers couldn't see in smoke, at night, and where we could we back-burned our tracks. By now we were the scorched and brittle texture of the bush around us. We nibbled the bodies of small charred animals — a spiny anteater, goannas — and vomited again. Steve and Joe chewed burned gumleaves to get the taste out of their mouths while Dan kept sucking rocks like they were toffees. It took an hour just to raise the spittle but then I ate my chinstrap. When at last we found another cave we killed two more horses to celebrate. We fell on their hot necks, pressed our faces in as if they were the iciest mountain streams.

Blood was the only food we could keep down. We drank six horses dry before we saw the croquet lawn three days later and guessed we'd live.

Coming close to Mrs C's property, we took the chance the bushfire had forced her husband and eldest son and men out mustering. Her Chinese laundry girl spotted us first but fled to the lavatory at the sight of these spirits of murder victims. Certainly we were a charnel house on legs. I – the scorched beast-creature in front – croaked after her, 'Get the missus!' and as the horses tottered to the water trough we peeled off their backs like scabs and pushed our snouts in alongside theirs.

Seeing us slobbering in the horse trough made her lose her colour. We weren't welcome with my lorikeet. First she sent her other children to their rooms. When she could speak properly she said, 'You're such a ghastly sight I wonder if I should shoot you for humanity's sake.' Both sides of her mouth now turned crisply down. She said, 'I didn't think anything could disgust me. I'm well travelled and a country woman and have seen many rough things in my life. But nothing like this.'

She shivered like she was the half-dead one while we shuffled like doomsday omens on the laundry floor. We were beyond shame or trousers. It wasn't just the blood and ashes clotting our hair and beards, our disgusting odours, our weeping organs, burnt, then chafed from riding. Our skins were layered stiff with blood, crackling and reeking, our mouths were crusted holes. Our blood-coats even had their own high noise: we hummed with flies.

I hadn't let on, but Joe blinked at her, then me, with ruptured eye veins from the smoke, and gave a sideways grin. '*Sunny days . . .*' he sang. He was croaking a banjo song of his and Aaron's, his eyes protruding like blood-reel marbles: '*Funny days. All our milk-and-honey days . . .*' Bow-legged little Steve, flyblown in several distant parts — maggots had begun to surface — stood deathly silent, bare feet splayed for balance and eyes squeezed shut, while she picked the wrigglers off him. Dan was the groggiest of us, made groggier by the medicinal brandy she'd brought out. Reeling and eyeing Mrs C, he tweaked his blackened prodder, saying, 'I don't suppose you'd go a spot of croquet?'

'You took a risk,' she hissed at me. 'Don't do that again.'

'I don't intend to,' I said. Didn't have the strength to laugh. I was feeling odd. Scrubbing and bathing gingerly, I was thinking how these blood-coats had soothed our burns and protected us in lieu of clothes. In a strange way I was loath to give mine up.

'Coming here, I mean,' she said. 'Phew, the smell of you. Like a badly slaughtered animal when they hit the bowels.'

Roar away, lion. Catch my smell on the breeze. Just another animal marking out its territory. And this is mine: this pool in the clay, these gum roots, the shine on those wet shadows, these weeds trampled by my nervy to-and-fro, that warm gust of sentimental human song.

Jesus, where's that train? Where's Hare? What's the time? Why aren't they here?

Wish we had our peacock here.

Why now these depressed and gutless moments? Keep thinking it's still not too late to end all this safely, for everyone to stay alive.

Alive or dead. It's not as if alternatives haven't been considered. Even canvassed this wild card: whisking off the Governor from the cosiness of his country residence at Mount Macedon.

I can see it now: Relax, Marquis, Lord, Your Excellency, dismiss your underlings and I won't lay a finger on you. Even though you've signed things to have me shot by total strangers, I'm doing this the civillest I can.

This is the scheme. How about a little man-to-man hard drinking in the ranges? Do you good to ride rough and shoot to eat, roll up in a blanket on the ground, wake up with frost silvering your mutton-chops. You can have a hearty bushman's breakfast — a spit, a piss and a good look round. Or, if you've got an appetite, wild figs and last night's leftover kangaroo-tail. Don't imagine you've drunk billy tea spiked with gumleaves and Irish whiskey, laughed around an open fire, smoked a pipe or two, exchanged the rudest gossip, given compliments where they're due.

And when each side's top dog has sniffed the other's bum we'll lay things on the table over brandy. A three-star conversation — the persecution of the Kellys, the mutual advantage of a bloodless give-and-take, the whole shebang. Jesus, Lord Normanby, let's face it, your mob's not very good at it. I've got all the selectors on my side: the country boys, the terrain, the whole bush telegraph. And the city people, the little people, don't mind me either. Hate to say this, Excellent, but we've got the numbers.

And don't worry, there's a precedent across the river. Your counterpart in New South Wales, Sir Hercules Robinson, pardoned Frank Gardiner on the condition he left the colony. And now I hear Frank's running the best saloon in San Francisco and a credit to all concerned.

Absolutely.

You can check with Sir Hercules. Drop him a line, send off a wire, give him my best.

Ha! Times change; we're out of fashion. It's thirteen years since they cut off Morgan's head and tied the corpse of Gardiner's mate, Ben Hall — carrying thirty-two bullets — to his horse and paraded it through the town of Forbes. God knows the precedents aren't good for outlawry.

Guess what, your Lordship. From our hideout at Bullock Creek, through intermediaries, I made them an offer at the outset. *Charge me and let her go.* The message came back along these lines: We don't bargain with outlaws — we'll catch you anyway. What do you think this is, son? That reminds us, must look in and see how your mother's doing. The word is that in between saying rosaries and Hail Marys she's looking after all the warders nicely, especially the Germans and those randy Orangemen. *Which one was your father, anyway?*

Okay for Gardiner, but Ben Hall was betrayed, first by his wife, then by a friend for money. Then ambushed by the police. Thirty-two bullets in his unarmed body. Over the years I took all that in.

Seems to be common practice everywhere. Read that Jesse James's brother Frank surrendered for an amnesty. Ended up an usher in a theatre. They had a sign: *Get Your Ticket Torn in Half by Former Outlaw Frank James.*

What about *my* brother? Looked at officially, the only ones who've personally killed anyone are me and Joe. Dan? Only a bit of assaulting here and there. Yes, sometimes Dan resents my orders, doesn't try to see the bigger picture. Doesn't appreciate my warnings about liquor. Says fugitives need their relief. 'Am I an outlaw or not? Correct me if I'm wrong, but if I'm not a man yet, why's half the country trying to shoot me, hang me, poison me, set my balls on fire?'

That sort of talk just makes me want to clip his ears. What's he thinking when he gallops off in a sulk, doesn't talk for hours and gets that younger brother's envious look?

Could Dan go against the blood? And his pal, Steve, he hasn't shot a soul. He could get an easy pardon for turning us in. Well, Jesus, what about Joe? My lieutenant, the man who knows the schemes. If I were Hare, Joe'd be the one I'd pardon to get the goods on us. Mustn't forget the one he killed wasn't police, just an informer. Just a paybook entry, easily overlooked if he turned state's evidence.

Just Aaron.

They could turn a blind eye to everyone but me. They could let the others go. Mother too. It's me they want to kill.

And I could call a halt to all this violence. Just blink and keep events from snowballing, at least stop the wild momentum. Four dead already, people gaoled and outlawed, a battle brewing. *A war!* All this madness happening now just because Alexander Fitzpatrick couldn't hold his brandy-and-lemonade!

Still not too late if we hurried. We could leave here this minute, singly or together. Saddle up and ride safely north across the border. Try a new life in Queensland, even New South Wales. Not as if we haven't swum the Murray before.

Then why don't we do it?

There's more to this now than me, or us.

— *Thank you. I will have another brandy. Just a small one.*

THE LADY that asked me about going straight — Madam, if it wasn't for Fitzpatrick, we'd be meeting in entirely different circumstances. No bonfires, lions and concertinas. Fitzpatrick changed the face of things for ever.

He's the pivot, the one in a hundred thousand who changes the way things are. Pity he's a liar and a fool. Things hardly ever work out neatly, do they?

It seemed like just an ordinary night at Eleven Mile Creek. Shepherd's pie. Everyone at the table but George King (absconded), Jim (out of gaol and shearing in the Riverina), and me. Me? I've been trimming Mrs C's bluestone foundations and am lingering late.

So Dan's the only male at home when Constable Fitzpatrick rides up by way of a nerve-settler at Lindsay's grog shanty with a warrant to arrest him for some horse matter. Thanks to the peacock's warning Dan is waiting on the doorstep, fork in hand, as he dismounts and states his business. Dan says, 'Very well, but let me finish my tea.'

Dan's story: Fitzpatrick sits down, sweating waves of brandy, keeps his hat on to look official but accepts a cup of tea while Dan slowly chews his pie, carefully butters a slice of bread right into the corners and stirs his tea relentlessly. All the kids around the table are agog at this infuriating performance. Snorts and muffled giggles, a fart or two. Mother frowns, the older girls sigh and roll their eyes.

Fitzpatrick slurps his tea and asks for something stronger. Kate brings him a rum and — the booze, the agreeable absence of other Kelly males — he gives her a drooling smile and tries to sit her on his knee. She elbows him. 'I'm sixteen and I'm not having that!'

Mother's reaching for the shovel. 'Let's see that warrant.'

Actually all he's got is a telegram from his district superintendent telling him to proceed with the serving of a warrant. He stands up, weaving, saying, 'He's arrested anyway,' and draws his revolver.

Chairs and dishes crash, the dogs jump for the shepherd's pie as mother swings the shovel at Fitzpatrick and swipes him on the helmet. But he gets his gun out, swearing bloody murder, so Dan yells, 'Here's Ned!' and as Fitzpatrick swivels around, clamps a wrestling hold on him and gets the gun. Dan throws him outside, taking the door with him, and on the way out Fitzpatrick scratches his wrist on the door latch.

And I'm riding home in a daze – still tingling from recent flesh events – unaware of all this. I'm snatching leaves off peppermint trees and munching them, rubbing the minty spittle on my face and neck (a guilty habit to throw my mother off the scent when I'd been with perfumed women), when I hear a horse coming up fast. I pull up behind a tree, and Fitzpatrick gallops past me in the opposite direction.

After the fight at our house he fled back to the grog shop and reeled home to the barracks at two a.m., spilling out his face-saving drama. Saying I'd been there and shot him in the *hand*. Even though the doctor who dressed the scratch would only say a bullet *might* have caused it, and that the patient stunk of brandy, his superiors jumped at this opportunity.

Attempted murder of a policeman by the Kellys! The suddenly, blissfully, dead-meat Kellys.

Can't reveal my alibi, that I was romancing Mrs C. So Dan and I ride off into the Wombat Ranges to Bullock Creek. Rewards posted on our heads. Mother's soon in gaol. All this is on the evidence of a single witness soon cashiered as a lying pisspot. Bugger the truth, they want me regardless. So angry, more than angry, I can't sleep or keep food down.

So I damn one woman by protecting another.

In a winter hiding guilty in the ranges the mind and body quickly turn to whisky.

WHISKY HANGOVERS have their good points. A rum hangover marinates the brain in syrup and overlays all next day, next week, with a sticky aftertaste. With a gin hangover it's shoosh the kids and hide the guns and mother's knives and draw the blinds and roll up in cotton sheets till the season changes. (Joe says a gin hangover is like looking at life through a black snake's bum. Inwards *or* outwards. Things are bleak and won't get any better.) Draw a pistol with a brandy hangover and you'll shoot something important off you. But a whisky hangover is like peering through a steamed-up window: it cuts out unnecessaries. Even the worst ones, where the bright world quivers behind clouds of leaves and feathers, can slowly set certain trains of thought in motion.

Bullock Creek's a good place to hide and think. For hiding and thinking and drinking – and for realising we have to make some quick, quiet money to get a new trial for our mother and a lawyer for ourselves. Deciding that a whisky still and gold digging are the quickest ways to make quiet money.

The Greta Mob helps us with a hut, two miles of fencing and cleared ground to grow barley and mangelwurzels to distil whisky. We've got all the tools for digging and sluicing for creek gold, and Tom Lloyd bringing regular news of police movements and sugar and extra supplies along the stock track over the hills from Greta. (Tinned herrings in tomato sauce for Dan, satsuma-plum jam for me.)

We build the hut strong enough to withstand a siege. Bulletproof logs two feet thick, an iron-plated door with loopholes to fire through. And from the hut we practise shooting in every direction with targets set up on trees at ranges from twenty to four hundred yards. Shoot and chop, shoot and chop. Shoot head and chest shots in the afternoon; every morning chop the cold bullets out of the wood, melt them down, remould them and shoot them again.

Spend one long winter among the gouged and

gradually splintering trees of Bullock Creek. Working on the stills and sluicing, selling gold dust, slaughtering the occasional footloose beast, socialising with trusted members of the Mob, practising our shooting every afternoon and preparing for the day when the police come for us.

Meanwhile we like the idea of being bootleggers, even building a dummy still in case of raids and hiding the main one downstream like all the best slygroggers. But we don't get to sell much whisky.

I'D LIKE to say in front of witnesses that I've got nothing against Kennedy. Seemed an honest man. I've never said he was a fool. Nor were we. Well . . .

He was the sergeant based at Mansfield. Discovered Tom Lloyd was regularly selling gold dust for someone and guessed Tom's cousins were hiding in the ranges. One of his informers had more details and told him the gang was hiding among the creeks. He'd seen Tom in the Greta general store. Look for a still, the spy said, prospectors' muddy tailings, a bit of barley crop. Jam and herring tins.

Stupid bugger didn't know enough to also warn him of the hut's wide radius of splintered trees, all gouged at the height of brain and heart.

Kennedy decided a pincer movement might flush us out – one party patrolling south from Greta and the other, led by him, searching north from Mansfield. A funny thing about police informers: as soon as Kennedy, Lonigan, Scanlon and McIntyre left town disguised as prospectors, the spy rapidly saw the other point of view and rode off to square himself with the Mob.

He was our informer too, you could say.

The showdown was brought on by exploding parrots. Rosellas. There was this explosion, then these booming, screeching echoes along the gulleys followed by a cloudburst of green and crimson steam.

What happened was this: Tom was already on his way out of town with the weekly supply of still-sugar, jam and herrings when Joe's mother waved him down at Twelve Mile Gully and passed on the informer's warning. Mrs Byrne didn't know how fast these phoney prospectors were travelling, only that they were heading in our direction. Tom galloped so fast along the stock trail his horse was roaring by the time he reached us. We reconnoitred and saw where their horses had stamped down the speargrass only a mile away at Stringybark Creek.

But there was no sign of them. I sent Tom to search downstream while Dan and I went upstream, keeping quiet and low. Joe and Steve followed ten minutes behind, to cover our rear. Still no sign of the police.

A perfect spot for snipers. But expecting a sneaky bullet makes any place seem ominous. Angled lumps of quartz poke from the hillsides here, and this particular afternoon these glistening outcrops looked to me like tilted gravestones. Long fluttery shadows fell across the creek. Breezes nipped around the ridges and hissed through the speargrass where it tangled up with the dense wattle and stringybark and sassafras trees down by the creek. Down here the visibility was down to twenty or thirty feet. And then this *boom* rang out and when its shock waves had echoed along the creek and our gullets had loosened enough to breathe again we saw shreds of feathers floating down like painted snowflakes.

McIntyre was the sort of sleuth-hound who eased his nerves by loosing two barrels at a flock of parrots. When the din and fluff had settled, Dan and I crept up to the police camp. It was very easy to find now, only two hundred yards away – as well as all his racket, McIntyre was by this time building a big smoky fire as a beacon to other members of the hunting party. There was a tent in the middle of a small clearing and another trooper was sitting by it on a log, daydreaming into the flames and twirling a revolver in his fingers.

Well, any real murderer would've picked them off from the bushes. A cinch for any monster! But my idea was just to take their guns and horses and leave them stranded. While Dan watched the man by the fire and I covered McIntyre, I stood up and ordered them to throw up their hands. Then things happened.

McIntyre did just as he was told.

The other man got clever and ran toward a pile of logs.

Dan froze and couldn't shoot him.

The man reached the logs. He raised his head to fire and I shot him through the temple.

The man said, 'Oh Christ, I'm shot!' and died.

I said, 'What a pity the bastard tried to run.'

I'm always quoted as saying that.

I KNOW the papers' name for it. *The Killers' Picnic*. Trooper McIntyre fussing around, boiling the billy, making tea and toast. And Lonigan the groin-grabber is spread-eagled, seeping, on the picnic rug. (You wouldn't read about it in the *Age*! Of all the police in Victoria I've killed the man I swore to kill!) While this fact sinks in I'm gulping strong tea so hot my tongue bubbles. And big, pale McIntyre's in a tizzy spreading fresh butter and marmalade on our slabs of toast.

He's offended when we make him taste the tea and food before us. He munches his toast in a huffy way, shakes his head at the very idea of poison. 'It's you who's the deathly worry to me,' he says. 'Not the other way round.' If we don't kill him he promises to leave the force first thing tomorrow. Of course all the time he's making toast, flattering our abilities and fervently decrying the police, he can't keep from casting sidelong glances at Lonigan's extra eye peering out.

The new eye is weeping colourless stuff. Well, no tears from me. If it has to be anyone's, I'm glad it's Lonigan's brain juices, that's all. Just look at it as my several-hundredth afternoon head-shot.

Dan's grinning at me. 'Very pretty.' Leans over and

picks a little red feather from my beard, and another. Bright parrot fluff sticking everywhere to me.

AT SIX the picnic ends suddenly. In the twilight the other police ride up from the west – Kennedy and Scanlon. I'm down behind a log; Joe and Dan crouch in the speargrass; Steve's in the tent. I'm covering our puppy-dog McIntyre as he steps into the sunset, saying, 'Sergeant, better surrender. You're surrounded.'

Kennedy's pink Irish bearded face, too well-groomed for any prospector, is still grinning at this joke – *Oh, Mac, ha ha . . . there's the welcoming fire, the cheery smell of toast!* – until I stand up and prove it. A general gasp, a split second passes – there's still just time for everyone to live a proper lifespan – but this time it's Scanlon who can't not try some cleverness. Swings his horse around, unslings his rifle, swings back and fires at me. So I shoot him in the heart.

At the far edge of the clearing, Kennedy's whipping out his revolver as he slides off his horse. Dan's advancing on him and Kennedy fires over the horse's rump and nicks Dan's left arm. Now Joe and Steve start blazing away from the shadows, so the gully's ripped by flashes, blasts, oaths and horse screams. It's almost dark. I can't get a clear shot at him. The panicky horse springs away and Kennedy fires into my face, so close I smell sizzled hair as the bullet parts my beard. McIntyre sees his chance, flings himself on his sergeant's horse and makes a run for it. And Kennedy stumbles toward the creek and crashes into the cover of the wattle and swamp gums.

I follow him.

This one's not an amateur. I've scooped up Scanlon's Spencer repeater but the mechanism's unfamiliar and I drop it in favour of my old shotgun. Kennedy retreats from tree to tree, stopping to fire, while I push him deeper and deeper into the scrub, trying to remember how many shots he's fired.

He fires his fourth shot (I think) ducking on the run, fifth (probably) from behind a tree. And he's aiming his sixth bullet (I estimate) when I hit him in the armpit with a blast of swandrops before he can fire.

When I shoot him in the armpit he drops his revolver and heads off again, crashing through the bushes in a shambling run. But at that second I don't realise he's dropped his gun. As he's changing his mind, panting like a croupy draughthorse and swivelling around to surrender, half-raising his arms in the twilight, I mistake the blood all darkening his hand for that revolver with one bullet left – and I fire again. And the shot passes through the right side of his chest.

In the new silence I move toward him through the crackling speargrass. Although he loudly argues that this is not the case, anyone can see he's had it. Hope he appreciates that it's not a proper topic for discussion. Embarrassing for both of us, his wheezy scoffing at those loose-petalled wounds like open roses, his begging and looking up at me like that. As an act of charity I position the gun between the two blooming roses, against his heart, and shoot him truly dead.

WE BURN the police tent without speaking and go back to Bullock Creek. Tired in my bones and head and legs, I feel my organs are all shrinking and withdrawing. At the same time my outline's flickering.

Skin's all shuddery; if you shook me I'd rattle like an old, loose-skinned kangaroo dog I once had. Rips from roos' claws and pigs' tusks letting in air pockets under Shandy's fur. A twitchy Great Dane—dingo cross — in the end Shandy sounded like his yellow flanks were packed with marbles.

My skin won't sit still on me.

The others: Dan's cross we didn't handcuff McIntyre — or shoot him; Joe's too cut up to speak, just smiles a vague smile and shakes his head now and then; Steve — all the way back to the hut Steve's gibbering how he's hungry, rambling on about lamb chops, steak and kidney pies, corned beef and brisket casseroles. But when we get there he can't even wait for meat to cook, so while the rest of us have big whiskies Steve sucks down five eggs instead.

'You two don't have to be in this,' I tell him and Joe. 'It's still only the Kellys. You can put yourselves in the clear, leave now — free as birds.'

Steve's poking his tongue around inside a shell for missed bits, and he grins up at me with yolk in his face-fluff. 'A short life and a merry one,' he says. You'd think this eggy kid was some rollicking high-wayman in a book.

'Well, tally-ho to you,' I say. 'It's New South Wales, then.'

Tom Lloyd keeps watch while we four try to snatch some sleep. Takes a bit of whisky to settle the flickering skin. After three hours we load two pack-horses, set fire to our bulletproof hut and get out of there.

It presses on my hip as I ride. The gold-rimmed circle. The watch. Christ, who needs another watch! Not a scratch on it, though.

The time's just after midnight. Fog rolls through the valleys of white quartz headstones, the creek is running deep and fast and rain starts hurling down.

For three days the rain pelts down and when they come out on to the Murray Plain the river is in flood. He sees that New South Wales has vanished and everything north of the Victorian bank churns under a muddy sea. Already dead sheep and cows and bush animals and sheds and trees and fences are whirling by in a stewy surge of topsoil. Two possums float past on their backs, legs outspread, neat genital purses exposed and vulnerable, and at once he thinks of his baby brothers, Danny and Jimmy, bobbing in their tin bath. *But now they're bony Dan and hairy Jim, who've been to gaol.* Big crows, their feathers in a sheen, flop along the crumbling loamy banks and eye the possums too.

He can't risk swimming the horses so they bring

them along a spongy length of bank to Bungowannah, to take the punt across. But their appearance — four armed, washed-out and wary horsemen on dog-tired mounts, and with laden packhorses — plus their apparent intention to make a border crossing in dangerous weather, attracts the attention of a middle-aged woman coming towards them in a pony trap. Despite the rain she gives them a close scrutiny, and the urgent way she trots her ponies up after she passes arouses his suspicions.

'Split up and we'll meet a mile back downriver,' he tells the others.

He guesses right about the informer. Only by tethering the horses among some field hacks in a muddy paddock and hiding in a lagoon do they escape the six-man police patrol that clatters down to the punt twenty minutes later.

So they spend three hours up to their necks in muddy water while the patrol splashes officiously back and forth along the bank. The police are uniformed and well-armed and their noisy orders carry over the water. There is much bold swearing and gesticulating in their oilskins and checking of guns and dispersing and trotting off through the puddles and then regrouping.

Perhaps they intend their voices to carry. Down in the lagoon the feeling is that the police will never make up their minds, also that some of them might be keener to keep the gang at a safe distance than to catch them. Up to their chins in ooze, they're grateful it's late October, with a hint of humidity in the north wind. Anyway, it's not much colder and wetter than being out in the weather. So they hide among the flotsam — well camouflaged too, with the four of them all soon as wrinkled and clay-stained as swamp-gum roots — until the patrol eventually rides off at dusk.

In the scummy eddies of the lagoon, platoons of ibises stride and peck and big groggy fish bob by. When they trudge out of the water at nightfall Dan and Steve scoop up two Murray cod each in their arms. These fish are monsters, three feet long. Gills full of muck, they're too stunned and soggy to fight or swim away.

'What do you want those bloody whales for?' the leader complains. 'We're nearly drowned and travelling light anyway.'

They're all shivering and waterlogged, but with silt clogging his eyebrows and browning his cheek-fuzz and downy moustache, his brother looks like some nappy water rat. Still he's beside himself, grinning while his teeth chatter. 'These cod are a delicacy,' Dans says, as proud as if he's caught them after a two-hour tussle. 'And getting rarer in the river with all the new steamboats churning about. They'll make a great meal on the other side.'

He feels like a weary parent, suddenly a generation older than this adolescent. And for that reason unable to refuse him. So, lugging cod, they squelch back to the horses, heave their bodies up, and ride back to the punt. It's unguarded now but resting on the bottom since the police have holed it. The fact starts sinking in that this exercise is more than just a search. It's a full-scale offensive. War has been declared.

'Forget New South Wales,' he says. They turn around and ride all night, cod thudding on their saddles, on side roads and stock tracks back into Victoria. They let the horses take their own pace, stopping only at dawn for food and shelter. Since his days on the prison hulk he doesn't eat fish, and after a close look at their cloudy eyes Joe, too, decides he needs only a warming whisky. So Dan and Steve polish off a half-grilled cod or two and aren't too sick.

Joe's old haunts are nearest. After three nights' hard riding they cross the range to Sebastopol, where his old friend Aaron Sherritt lives. At this stage of his life Aaron is still a bachelor living in a slab hut on his parents' farm. Joe insists it's a safe house and that the Sherritts are no lovers of the police.

'The Sherritts aren't Catholics – Old Man Sherritt's a fucking Orangeman!' Dan says.

'Relax,' Joe says. 'John Sherritt's always before the courts for some bastardry or other. Anyway, Aaron's engaged to my sister. Jesus, you know he's an old mate of all of you boys.'

The Sherritts take them in. Their hut is like a musty cave – no windows, and the only light and air comes through the open doors. Of course Aaron is keen to drink and sing and play his banjo but they're so bushed they just roll up in their dank blankets under Old Man Sherritt's prized portrait of Queen Victoria. This is before she's made proclamations to have them killed, but even now she's looking down her nose at them, those puffy little cod eyes following them around the tiny room like Jesus' moist spaniel ones did from the wall above Mother's bed.

They lie down to rest with the Sherritts' eyes on

them too. It's only noon after all. Father and son are lunching at the table and well into the bottle they've been given. Aaron is singing some flattering made-up song about dead troopers and Stringybark Creek while Old Man Sherritt is munching lamb shanks and water biscuits with his whisky, cleaning his Enfields – a breechloader and an old muzzle-loading musket – and reminiscing about his days as a rip-roaring corporal in the Royal Irish Constabulary. In this ruckus their collie bitch scrapes her way indoors and towards the table. She's dragging her hind legs along the rectangle of sunshine from the doorway; ticks have paralysed her and made her eyes gluey. She looks up through this slimy film at Sherritt senior, sighs and folds herself into three stiff sections – legs, body, head – at his feet.

Spitting biscuit crumbs, Old Man Sherritt booms, 'Oh, we used these old boys, didn't we?' and pats his musket lovingly. The whisky's already turned his cheeks all friendly. 'When the British Army got their new breechloaders they passed over these old gadgets bloody quicksticks to the Royal Irish. Well, we got some Tykes with them anyhow.'

'Olden days, Pop. Long gone,' Aaron says, plunking on.

The leader clears his throat and opens an eye. 'Joe?' he murmurs.

'Four tired Tykes right here, Mr Sherritt,' Joe says. 'But we've all got wide-awake Colts under our blankets.'

Sherritt blinks, and frowns as if something important has just occurred to him. ''Course they had their misfiring difficulties and slownesses,' he goes on, laying the musket on the table with a rosy smile. 'Otherwise we wouldn't have taken such a shine to these,' he says, picking up the other weapon, sighting along the barrel, putting it to the collie's velvet ear and firing.

Immediately they're at the table, stumbling in their socks and underwear, slipping in dog blood, unsure where to point their Colts. Aaron's father is already resting the rifle across his knees and pinching his waxed moustache tips — orange from tobacco and already turned up smartly — into new assertive points.

'Daddy, she might've got better!' Aaron says.

'We'll never fucking know,' says Old Man Sherritt, reaching for another shank.

They decline the Sherritts' offer of overnight shelter and at dark they rouse themselves from the floor and ride across the flooded Oxley Plains with four new horses Aaron has picked up from the Mob, their other four as spares and two pack animals. Riding beyond their exhaustion, they move through Everton and Wangaratta after midnight and head up into the thickly forested hills and crevices of the Warby Ranges. The land is drier here, and safely rugged, safe enough for them to keep riding into the crisp morning.

In the thermals whistling kites soar in pairs, buoyant and easy, then drop, shrieking, after rabbits. Sun glances off the granite shelves where black snakes and copperheads have come out to bask in new skins. Dizzy in its glare, they climb higher into the hills, gritty eyes drawn every so often to those tall and isolated ghost gums topped by wedge-tailed eagles' nests, boldly conspicuous platforms seven, eight feet across, with clear views of the surrounding territory. Rounding a bluff, they come upon one wedge-tail tearing at a dingo pup. Everyone stops, hands drop automatically to guns but, strangely, no one shoots. Then the day extends into a frozen moment of fierce defiance, a frowning standoff, before the eagle grips its meal and the party shakes off its self-consciousness — its leaden, human foreignness – and watches it start arrogantly into the sky. It trails long streamers of fur and entrails. Its claws grip without mercy but how admirable the languorous way its wing tips caress the air.

It's now November, the favourite pale-yellow time of early summer, and they're back in a place they know well and which is well aware of them.

FLAME

For six weeks after Stringybark all this summery country becomes a black and white Inferno, and he the Devil.

From city desks and drawing boards come dramatic representations, in words and pictures, of the sombre ravines and precipices, the jagged crags and scars of the monster's territory. This is Hell's gaseous fire lifted holus-bolus from the depths and thrust into the tender and defenceless features of Victoria. And there in the centre of the holocaust stands Satan with his eyebrows meeting in the middle, eyeteeth glistening and shotgun smoking.

That is the view from Melbourne. Meanwhile Satan is drinking ale in a hammock in the hills with his shirt off and his eyes and ears open. He's reading the papers and listening to cicadas.

He takes in all the rumours and ballyhoo. They've escaped to New South Wales, South Australia, America – no, the Cape of Good Hope. A Sydney shipmaster swears he sold them tickets to Cape Town. They plan to storm Pentridge prison and rescue his mother. He's gathering an army of angry rural selectors and city workers to overthrow the government and found the Republic of Northern Victoria. *Is he, indeed?*

And while he takes the dry and drowsy air, the press is lecturing the government and Chief Police Commissioner Standish on sparing no expense to run the murderers to earth, blah blah. In other words, Standish should pull his finger out and it wouldn't hurt his men to do the same.

The papers abuse the police for creeping in tentative circles around the places they'd been spotted. First, Superintendent Nicolson had set out to catch them on the Murray riverbank, sending a party of troopers on ahead, then dispatching himself to the border by first-class train. (When he arrived, his cheerful blacktrackers reckoned they had only missed the gang by a fortnight.) Then, after two days' cautious ruminating,

Inspector Brooke Smith had led twenty-two troopers out from Wangaratta into the foothills of the ranges. But coming across a lame packhorse the gang had left behind (Brooke Smith saw its police brand – it was Lonigan's horse, taken at Stringybark Creek), such unpleasant premonitions came to him that he'd ordered his men straight back to barracks.

So when a sighting is reported at the Sherritts' hut at Sebastopol, Chief Commissioner Standish decides to stop this rot and – as soon as he's fulfilled his social obligations at the Melbourne Cup – lead the troops himself. Maybe it was the association with a famous British victory. *His own Charge of Sebastopol!* To bolster his twenty police he even deputises thirty civilians, mostly wealthy squatters. But not all.

And so reports travel the other way as well, to the man in the hammock. Of the police and vigilantes riding through the night to the shack at Sebastopol. Of Chief Commissioner Standish watching from the brow of the hill, like the noblest general, while Nicolson leads the midnight charge recklessly down the slope, rampaging through the Sherritts' rocky home paddock and through their marshy creek and up to their hut. Of Nicolson throwing himself off his horse and bursting through the door, bumping Constable Bracken, whose gun went off. Of all the other troopers and steamed-up amateurs, excited by the gunshot, crowding inside too, fifty armed panickers cramming into this twenty-by-twenty-foot hut, cursing and waving their rifles and trying to strike matches in the dark and overturning the Sherritts' furniture and pulling blankets off their beds looking for outlaws.

And of there being no one there, not a dog to bark, not even a Sherritt. (The gang, of course, hadn't been there for six or seven days.)

Of the police, frustrated but still fired up, then unsuccessfully raiding the Byrnes' house and being sent packing by Joe's indignant mother.

Of the Sherritts next morning marching up to the by now exhausted police party, the old man in high indignation, complaining of the attack on the home of such a loyal Queen's man.

And of Aaron, in quite a different mood (appearing, according to observers, urbane and confident and affecting the rounded tones of the rural aristocracy), approaching the Chief Commissioner for a chat.

I can't hear myself think! Someone rouse Orlando and tell him the lion wants feeding. And stop his monkey doing that — there's ladies and children present!

— *Did you hear what Dan here said? Monkey reminds him of Sir Redmond Barry when he goes at it hammer and tongs like that.*

Hello, hello, listen up just a minute while I read out this cutting from the *Police Gazette*. This is a list of the field equipment issued to each trooper engaged in what the government likes to call the Hunt (exclusive of uniform and weaponry of course):

Two rugs, a rolled blanket, a spare undershirt and drawers, two pairs of socks, a valise, two shirt collars, a comforter, one cloth and one waterproof topcoat, leggings, a hammock, a sheet of waterproof, a tent 6 feet by 8 feet, books, a lantern, a bush knife, cutlery, cup and dishes, spare trousers, spurs and an air pillow.

Grog and food also not included. Or the strychnine, arsenic and bribe money. Or what I hear's the newest anti-Kelly thrill: the cannons.

But, see, they're all as snug as bugs in rugs. Just the ticket for comfy riding in the country on double pay, for seducing country girls, for moving up and down the railway line at a gentlemanly distance from the enemy. That way you don't get to be another Kennedy.

Reckon they could all do with a bullet in their air pillows.

— Just top it up, thanks, Mrs Jones. Same again for everyone! No, I won't join in the chorus — a little hoarse — you go ahead though.

No more sherry for Judge Barry, he's inflamed enough already.

SEEMS LIKE peanuts now, the first reward for Dan and me. Eight hundred pounds. The Government recalling Parliament especially to pass something called the Outlawry Act. Placing the Gang beyond the normal protection of the law. (Any member of the Gang could be shot by anyone at any time; anyone assisting us faced gaol and they'd throw away the key.) The reward going up to two thousand — and rising.

Christ, the onslaught. All the city and country papers publishing summonses calling on us to surrender by November 12th. Printing details of the Act on handbills and papering them across the state. Nailing up *Wanted* posters for the Mob to pull straight down.

And the law turning its attention on Pentridge prisoners who'd known us, making them certain promises. Bill Williamson believing we'd flee into New South Wales through the Buffalo River Valley, detouring to the town of Lurg to collect supplies. Mick Woodyard telling them Joe was certain to be a member of the Gang. Advising them to watch the route from the Wombat Ranges through to Barwidgee, then to Barnawartha and Howlong, believing we'd cross the Murray at the Bungowannah punt. Not far wrong, Mick, just a bit late off the mark.

Plaguing our friends and family. Arresting Wild Wright and his brother Tom for threatening language and locking them up, their lawyer pointing out that Tom is better known as Dummy Wright. Being deaf and dumb, he doesn't use language threatening or otherwise.

And all this time spying on my sisters. Shadowing them every time they leave the house. Laying strychnine baits for their dogs so the yapping wouldn't give their spies away. So Maggie's and Kate's dogs wear muzzles day and night. And the girls start walking them on leashes, four or five muzzled dogs each, up and down outside the Benalla police station just to drive them crazy. Mad Nicolson even convinced Maggie sends us messages in her washing. The way she hangs clothes on the line must signal things. Right-side-up trousers means it's safe, he thinks; upside-down trousers means troopers coming; the number of socks hanging up is the number of miles away.

'Well, long johns with the back flap open must mean officers,' Joe says.

Maggie then enjoying hanging pants up sideways, shirts dangling by one arm, a line full of corsets.

'Watch it you aren't gaoled for hanging insulting washing,' I tell her.

LOVE TO drive them crazy. Love to amuse ourselves by tracking the search parties out tracking us. This is a cinch, the way they toss away their empty rum bottles and beef tins and snap twigs off trees to pick their teeth and leave pyramids of shit behind every second bush. A mystery to me why they don't use the blacktrackers more. (All right by me!) The blacks are so good they make my blood run cold. It's because they're so good they don't use them; they don't want to be shown up. Funny people, police.

Drives them crazy that we haven't let the Hunt cramp our style. They call this being *flash*, and now the press has picked up the word. Meaning cockiness and not kowtowing to stuffy English expectations. *Flash* is attending the Whorouly races as usual, playing billiards with Wild Wright, going home to Joe's for dinner – entering the house using Wall's Gully – right under the noses of the watching police, and visiting Melbourne regularly to mingle with the horsey set and buy good guns. (Did get a fright, though, wandering around the Melbourne Exhibition, my pockets stuffed with apples, to see Higgins, the Beechworth magistrate, staring straight at me. Not as surprised as Higgins, however, seeing me and my apples jump into a cab and disappear into Bourke Street.)

Flash is me secretly marrying Steve's sister and Joe's sister and a housemaid in Deniliquin with the exotic name of Madela – or would be if I'd done it like the *Chronicle*, the *Advertiser* and the *Argus* said.

Can't see myself being that flash.

Rivers fall again, seasons turn, people suddenly start to crack a smile and wink a certain way and straighten up when they talk about you. Even a lot of our enemies changed their minds about us as soon as we robbed banks.

Maybe they admired us for acting out their own wishes. Who doesn't daydream of robbing a bank, of staging a neat, well-mannered crime?

Like clockwork.

Six weeks after Stringybark the Murray is running low enough to cross — so the police are reminded in a letter from my uncle, Pat Quinn, which falls deliberately into Constable Flood's mail-tampering hands. Uncle Pat's letter provides dates and details of our next attempt to cross the border. So Superintendents

Nicolson and Sadleir hurry to the river to set up a joint trap with the New South Wales police. And so with the police strength of the region trotting north, we canter south towards Euroa.

Steve's not yet recognised as a gang member so I send him into town to reconnoitre the National Bank position. We know that next Tuesday is the day the licensing court sits in the Town Hall, keeping the town's only constable occupied. Steve comes back saying that the side door of the bank is kept ajar between 3.30 and 4 p.m. when the railway master deposits his takings. And that Scott, the bank manager, and his family live on the premises.

Clockwork.

We need a staging point for this exercise. On Monday at noon we saunter into Younghusbands' station four miles north of Euroa, bail up the station-hands as they come in to lunch, lock everyone in the storeroom, and keep them cheerful enough with food and Dan's saucy pack of cards while we eat lamb and chutney sandwiches in the kitchen.

But only after the housekeeper's tasted them first. My usual worry about strychnine and arsenic. 'Nothing personal,' I say to her. 'Do you know Dan Morgan wouldn't eat anything but boiled eggs in company, and he wouldn't eat those if they were cracked?'

Must say she doesn't look as if she wants to poison us. Keeps smiling at us with her shallow, dish-shaped face. We've never looked or smelled more spruce, thanks to a hawker named Gloster who blithely drove up just behind us in his covered wagon and quickly joined the prisoners in the storeroom while we took turns to outfit ourselves from his best stock. Now everyone's flash as a rat with a gold tooth: new whipcord trousers, tweed jackets and waistcoats, soft cotton shirts, the best quality felt hats and English riding boots. And we've sprinkled eau de cologne on our new silk cravats. We're the most stylish murdering thieves northeastern Victoria's ever seen when, next afternoon, we leave Joe overseeing the captives' card game, chop down the telegraph poles along the railway, drive the hawker's wagon and the farm's springcart into Euroa and rob the National Bank of everything it's got.

We've brought the carts to take Scott the banker and his family as prisoners. When we slip inside their residence they're all dressing for a funeral. The wife's a tall, good-looking, bony woman who recovers smartly from the shock of us. He calls her Susan. Despite our guns and need to hurry, Susan Scott insists that mourning wear is unsuitable for a hostage travelling in the countryside. 'I'm not going any distance wearing black in summer like a grandmother,' she says, and demands to change into a creation just arrived from Melbourne. The boys and I exchange looks while she sails into her bedroom. We're worried she'll signal from her window, so while she changes clothes we leave her door open a crack and I get Steve to stand just outside.

Like to be a fly on the wall of that room myself but something bloody-minded makes me turn aside. How to tell if some woman stirs me: I'm the pig-headed, frowning one standing farthest away.

The way her husband's afternoon has gone so far has set him pacing up and down and made him pallid and moist around the hairline. The chunky sort, quick to sweat and anger. After ten minutes waiting he and I catch each other's eye. 'Whisky?' I say. So we have a glass. (After he's tasted it first.) Then there's a sigh and crash and we need more whisky for his wife's old nurse, who's fainted at all her nightmares becoming real. And for her mother, who says with all this excitement she needs a heart starter too.

After half an hour Susan Scott makes her entrance in fancy muslin and lace and ribbons, long white driving gloves and a hat covered with tulle and paper flowers. 'Well?' she says.

Women with tickets on themselves usually make me act thick, pretend not to get their drift. Annoys me that they appeal the most.

'Well, are we all ready now?' I say.

She twirls with a little frown. And looks questioningly along her narrow nose at me.

By now, on this worst day of his life, Scott's looking redder and ropable. No need to make it worse. 'Not quite what I expected,' I say.

'You're not either,' she says. 'A magenta cravat! The *Age* said you looked distinctly animal, with the facial features of a creature born to crime. They also called you a mutilator of the dead.'

'I wouldn't believe that tripe.'

Dan pipes up, 'He can be a handful though.'

'Are you the brother?' she says. 'I wouldn't wear yellow with your skin.'

We get still more than we bargained for. We have to abduct all the family. We can't leave anyone behind to give the alarm so into the carts we load the Scotts and their seven children, then help up Susan Scott's mother – a big woman also – and her old nurse with the vapours, and then their two servant girls, putting four children in one cart and three in the other as a security precaution. Then there's the three of us to squash in somewhere. I give Susan Scott the reins of the springcart. I drive the wagon, with Dan keeping a gun on her from a hole cut in the wagon's canvas.

We also take a freshly baked cake from the Scotts. (And the robbery proceeds.)

As we pass the cemetery (someone's child has died) Susan Scott is horrified at what the funeral party will think of her driving past in unseemly haste. But as we leave the last shacks behind and ride into the yellow countryside, the open air soon flushes along her high and sharp-boned cheeks. She has emphasised a mole above her top lip, just above and to the side of the cupid's bow. She'd be maybe forty, bland-skinned for her age; reminds me of a flouncier version of Mrs C. She glances sidelong at me, has to shout above the cicadas' buzz, the wheels and horses. 'What are you going to do with us now?'

'Madam,' I yell back, 'we're taking you out to tea.'

We arrive back at Younghusbands' station where

we make a ceremony of burning the selectors' mortgages, take tea with the Scotts, swap Dan's horse for a
superior Younghusband bay gelding and entertain
our guests with some trick-riding. One by one we
boys stand on the saddle, one by one we bend to pick
up her handkerchief, race each other the length of the
home paddock. She's laughing, we're laughing, getting
hot faces, showing off. Only when the evening's first
mosquitoes begin to bother Susan Scott's canny
cheeks do we simmer down. We load the treasure on
to our pommels. We put on frowns and order everyone to sit tight for two hours under pain of ghastly
death. And then we ride off, laughing like devils and
jumping fences, into the bluish, fading light.

NOT QUITE true. I did look. For a long moment I
peered into the crack of her bedroom doorway. I sent
her husband off with Dan for whisky and I looked.
My ears roaring with this new excitement – power,
success – and an urge to glimpse forbidden things. A
shadowed light spilling along the corridor – a gentler

light than enters huts. Patterned sun squares burnishing the walls and carpet. The day vibrating outside. What I saw in this powdery female air was her dressing table and on it a wide, white bowl of objects. A display of her treasures. Egg-shaped river stones of many sizes, notched and gashed with red streaks of iron, lumps of quartz veined with fool's gold, pyrites, also wild birds' eggs – spotted, white and blue, from magpies to emus. And, tastefully arranged among them, a selection of small skulls.

The bank manager's wife collected the skulls of wallabies, possums, koalas, a bandicoot, something even smaller – maybe a tiny shrew or two. A perfumed bowl of eye sockets and grimaces. They looked well handled. It dawned on me that these small skulls were egg-shaped too.

Another flare spears up into the sky from Dray's Peak. They're still in place and waiting but they're wondering now. Getting impatient. Where's the bloody train, what the Christ's happening? With this noise, the singing, the concertina, have we missed the whistle? I've even forgotten how a train whistle sounds. Getting tired of always waiting for some whistle or other, some flagman's-warder's-lookout's-scout's-spy's-watchdog's-peacock's signal on what the next stage of my life will be.

Used to lie awake in the dark hut waiting for his homecoming whistle. *Wheep-whew.* Every night he'd whistle coming through the door. Never mind the time, all hands on deck. Every available child running and greeting him by the dying note of that *Wheep-whew.*

I would still run, but warily.

Strange: as his body gradually filled with liquid, the whistle dried up. Lost its juicy warble. At the end it had that lonely piping sound.

Now I can't waver, must stay like gristle, like tendon. Pliable but firm. Must stay calm and think clearly. *Stay like gristle* was a favourite expression of old Harry Power's. Didn't lack gristle or guts, Harry, just basic grey matter.

Wait and listen, stay calm. Sometimes best to let events adjust around you. Things do make room for you — nature, air, even rocks sometimes. Like when we rode back through the black landscape beyond Benalla after the last time I saw Mrs C up close.

No bird, insect or frogthing chirping, even the bushflies dead or gone. In the scorched silence we make a different sight from our arrival, four saner ghosts, riding a horse each, our naked heads and chins all sickly luminous against the trees.

We've shaved off our burnt and crusty hair. Mrs C's fed, watered, clothed and patched us up, but only after we've pulled pistols on her. That makes the situation more comfortable for her. Another advantage of the guns: they enable us to select better horses than would have been on offer otherwise.

'You're not taking Princess Beatrice!' This is her husband's favourite hunter, a lovely grey mare named after Queen Victoria's youngest, only a six-year-old and with her best hunting years still ahead of her. Mrs C speeds after me into her stall, swings the feed bucket against my shin, then tries to snatch my Colt. Luckily the Princess has learned manners from an early age, is trained not to kick out at hounds; she doesn't lift a gracious hoof for the fifteen or twenty minutes we roll underneath her in the straw.

'This is where you belong,' says Mrs C.

'In you?'

'In the dung and muck.'

My shaved, pale head certainly makes me look like something wormy from under a stone. With all my burns and grazes smarting, I'm moving sluggish like one too.

'I thought you'd moved up in the world to murderer,' she says, 'but you're still a shitty horse thief.'

'I'll probably get the mare back to you,' I say. 'Though it won't do your husband any harm at all to lose it to me.'

As we argue under her we slowly start to rub and rustle in the straw. The lines around her eyes and mouth, her frowning years, smooth out. Although awake I dream I'm describing perfect circles. A kick, a braining death, don't bother me. Finally my blistered fingers tip the pulse. Concentrate all my scabby flesh on this last humming gentleness. As it happens, even birdcalls between her legs don't worry serene Princess Beatrice.

So I ride the Princess away into the smell of charred trees, through the forest of smoking splinters. She's already the colour of fine ash. Branches of black banksia nuts like cremated monkeys droop over us. Even the thinnest mosses and palest lichens haven't escaped the fire. Every wisp and bud and sound of life is scorched and crisped away. The whole land looks like toasted death, the very End.

In a silent line the four of us ride back into our territory. At least now the smoke has died away the visibility is good. After a bushfire you can see and hear a police patrol ten miles away unless they're blacktrackers. At sunset we camp on a high elephant-shaped rock still warm from the fire and the sun. The missing evening bird choir, the void of the crickets, the total blackness, suddenly begin to weigh on us. We lie spread-eagled on the rock. Everyone is more or less normal again, but we can't raise the spirit to speak or eat. The bushfire-sun sets gauzy red, the moon rises yellow as a guinea, the Southern Cross sparks down. The sky is the only light and movement and form of conversation.

The sky wakes us at sunrise and we eat some supplies from Mrs C's. Our food crumbs make ants appear instantly from nowhere. And as we gaze dully at the blackness the faintest tips of colour catch the corners of our eyes — exciting, sappy shoots are sprouting from burnt tree trunks; shiny maroon, green and purple leaves are bursting out. At the edge of our hearing a magpie, or its echo, calls. The pink flush in the sky rims the eastern cloudbanks and then flares gold. The overhead sky swings from sulky grey to blue like it was never otherwise.

I GET a contact to leave one hundred guineas from the Euroa haul in Mrs C's name at the front desk of the Commercial Hotel and I keep Princess Beatrice for myself.

What's a little guilt compared to a good horse? She's the best I ever stole — and she's got two hundred and eighty-three to beat. Certainly the best I ever paid for, and even worth the money. Sweet, randy memories every time I ride her. Anyway, she deserves a more exciting life than carrying a rich farmer's arse after the mangy offspring of English foxes.

And I think Mrs C could have minded more. That day in the stable my knee hit on something hard. A little Allen & Thurber .32 revolver hidden in the folds of her dress.

'Are you going to shoot me with that pepperpot?' I say.

And she says, 'Now I know I easily could have, that's enough.'

Jerilderie is the mare's and my next adventure together. The mood we're in there decides what I call her. *Mirth.*

After Euroa there was pressure on Standish to put a new man after us. He chose Superintendent Francis Augustus Hare, his assistant commissioner, a South African and, like himself, a 'man of fashion' and member of the Melbourne Club. Then he told Hare to sign up this charming young informer who'd made himself known to him.

We'd been wondering about Aaron for a while. We all wanted to know for sure. Joe wanted to give him a second chance because he'd just got married. So Joe and Dan rode up to Aaron's new selection opposite the Sugarloaf for a matey chat. Joe squatted on the ground for a heart-to-heart, sucked a piece of grass, drew a map in the dirt with a stick. (Aaron's new wife was too young and green to invite them inside, or even offer a cup of tea. Dan stayed on his horse. He didn't trust Aaron even then.) Joe told Aaron, well, we're going here, and then here, to Goulburn in New South Wales to rob a bank and we want you to act as scout. Aaron excused himself, just being married and so forth. Winked at his old friend. Joe said never mind and he and Dan rode off.

Waited a few days. (Joe had given nothing away, since we actually intended heading towards the Riverina.) When Hare tightened security and poured men into the northeast we knew Aaron was seriously on the job.

Running from Victoria, Dan Morgan reached the Murray along the Warby Ranges, outwitting the police for the last time before they took his head on tour. Splitting into pairs two hours apart, we follow Morgan's route twelve years later and come down onto the blood-red claybank downstream of Yarrawonga on a dry and humming February afternoon. The river trickles as slow as rust. In the heat we swim the horses across to the New South Wales side and climb up on the scrub plain without sighting anything human.

Jerilderie has five pubs, one for every fifty people. First and last in the main street is the Woolpack Inn, a bloodhouse where Mary Jordan runs the bar and keeps track of local police movements, the whereabouts of

Sergeant Devine and his constable, Richards. Joe sweet-talks her while we drink and eat, still in pairs and incognito, Joe and Dan together, Steve and me, pretending not to know each other. Until we join up outside just before midnight.

A hammering on his door. Wake up, Devine, wake up. There's been a murder at the Woolpack!

Devine weaves onto the verandah, blinking awake, Richards hurrying to join him, grumbling and buckling on their belts. Some bastard on a grey horse doing the yelling. Jesus, come quick!

Christ, not the Woolpack again, Devine says.

Then three men suddenly behind him, pointing guns. The horseman wheeling his mare and coming at them fast, levelling a Colt. Kelly! Devine says. Correct, sergeant. The Gang handcuffs them, pushes them into their own cells with the Saturday night drunks.

Steve, still hungry of course, orders Mrs Devine to cook us a meal. Then I take first watch while the others sleep. In the night a tired voice from the cells: Thanks for rooting my career.

SUNDAY IN Jerilderie. Ninety in the dusty shade, the hot air suspending specks of harvest chaff. All blinds drawn in the sergeant's residence to discourage heat and visitors. In the darkened sitting room the chairs and sofa wear stiff covers; no one ever sits here. In a corner a big glass case of brightly-coloured stuffed birds of the region. Sergeant Devine's hobby is trapping them with nets and birdlime. Another is collecting pistols, some of them with funny enough calibres and barrels to hang on the wall: muzzle-loaders, a twelve-shot .38, a Winburn single-shot .65 percussion pistol, a Tranter six-shot .45 with octagonal barrel, a .41 revolver like Ben Hall's. The way she twitches and wrings her hands, she wants us out of there. I say I'm just checking none of these trinkets is loaded. Just stay out of the sitting room and I'll cooperate, she says. No, don't open that. Don't let that hot wind in on the parrots!

Something else is bothering her. She always prepares the Courthouse for Mass — no Catholic church here — so Dan lends a hand, carries the flowers across the street for her. Poppies, carnations, bunches of maidenhair and stag ferns. Helps arrange them, comes back looking soulful with a carnation in his lapel.

Steve, meanwhile, has the oven stoked, the leg of lamb coated with lard, salted and peppered and sitting in the baking dish. He's peeled and sliced the potatoes, pumpkin, carrots and parsnips and shelled the peas. By now he's sweating, dripping on the table, leaving a trail across the floor and food, and chopping mint leaves for a sauce. Where've you been? he says — *chip chop* — I've been working my fingers to the bone.

Joe and I can't stop laughing, almost splitting our uniforms. (Devine and Richards are built narrower than us.) We're dressed up as police, having given Richards an empty revolver and gone on his peace-keeping rounds with him (especially noting arrangements at the Bank of New South Wales), telling everyone we're special reinforcements sent to guard Jerilderie against the Kellys. We've visited the blacksmith and had our horses re-shod, charged it to the police account and shouted Rea, the blacksmith, a drink at the Royal Mail Hotel. An important drink. The Royal Mail abuts the bank.

MONDAY. AT noon Jerilderie's a street of slow-moving shapes. Horses, carts and occasional verticals crossing obliquely from shade to shade. Still in uniform but this time with revolvers unholstered, we return to the Royal Mail, round up the manager, staff and customers, herd them into the bar-parlour and leave Steve guarding them while Dan watches the pub's street entrance. He gives any thirsty customer a sharp count of three to jump the counter and join the prisoners.

Then Sergeant Byrne and Constable Kelly stroll next door into the bank and hold it up. No trouble from the astonished accountant, name of Living, or young Mackie, the clerk. The manager, Tarleton, is missing. Living says he's upstairs changing after a dusty business journey.

Well, Tarleton's soaking in his bath and shocked and shy to see us. When we come through the door – Joe and me with guns and the two bank johnnies, all crowding in the bathroom – he sits up in a flurry, eyes wide and white, grabs a flannel to cover his bobbing whatsis, then looks around for weapons and brandishes an uncertain loofah.

Hope that sponge isn't loaded, Joe says, heh heh.

It takes a pair of trousers, a dressing gown and

smoking cap to make Tarleton managerial. Downstairs in the bank he insists there's only six or seven hundred pounds in the safe. He's only underestimated by five thousand. While he's dickering, the local schoolteacher, Elliott, comes into the bank and when he's recovered I get him to hold open a sugarbag while I throw in all the sovereigns and sterling and all the other gold and silver coins. Then get him to write out a notice giving the children a holiday in honour of my visit.

The bloody bank's as busy as Flinders Street Station. Next the town's leading citizen, J.D. Rankin, comes in with Samuel Gill, the newspaper proprietor, and a storekeeper named Harkin, and raps on the counter for service. From Tarleton's office I call out, I'll be right with you. Then I jump out, banging my revolver butts down with a clatter. Don't move! I catch Rankin and Harkin, but Gill jumps over Rankin and runs away. Take the others to the Royal Mail with the other prisoners. I need a drink, need to tie up loose ends.

By now we don't need to point guns at people. In the bar I clap a revolver on the counter, swearing if anyone tries to shoot us or send a telegraph, Jerilderie will swim in its own blood. Then I call the barmaid for drinks all round. My shout, Lovely. Just take it out of these new sovereigns here.

Leave my gun sitting there on the bar. People leave it be. It's as if it were a person, sitting there with its own air space around it. Wouldn't be surprised to see someone buy it a drink.

TYING UP loose ends takes time. Joe's sticking up Jefferson the postmaster, checking all the telegrams sent this morning, cutting the wires on the switch-board. I leave the pub to chop down two telegraph poles, am looking sideways at a third when a local man named Charlie Naw volunteers to chop it for me, and goes on to chop another six. Wires springing and tangling everywhere in the street. Buy willing Charlie a drink while I'm waiting for Joe. One thing's still bothering me: the newspaperman, Gill.

I'm told he lives across from his printery, so I front up to his doorstep. His wife denies he's there, says he's probably lying somewhere, dropped dead with fright. Can't see anything ever frightening her, or interesting her either. Looks just to the side of me, not straight on, as if I was a scurvy sore, perhaps, a bad case of cowpox. I say there's something I want to give him. Joe and I have been working on it for three months. I hand her this bag of papers I've been carting around ever since. Will you pass it on? It's important to me. Not possible, she says. I thought it might be interesting, I say. It's begging to be printed. Afraid not, she says, looking somewhere over my shoulder as if at approaching inclement weather.

So we leave. Take our new treasure, mount up and ride out of town in four directions to confuse them.

What I wanted to give her news-hound husband was this story of my life.

He must stay awake, keep moving about, listen for the train. With all the planning, killing Aaron, the long ride here, the taking of prisoners, the entertainment, the waiting, none of them has slept or even lain down with his boots off for three nights. Dropping off for only a moment on the verandah step just now, he instantly dreamed he was lounging with friends on a fine, clipped lawn.

Around them, strolling strangers chatted and took the air. He found himself beginning to dig tunnels in the neat lawn and undermining it. All these mild people strolling past fell into the holes, which filled quickly with water. But he and his friends ran for the high ground, a grassy hill topped by a timber, bark-roofed hut, and were safe and snug there. They felt lucky and gifted, especially as all the people in the holes quickly drowned.

But then there was a knock on the door. With some apprehension he opened it and there was his father as a young man, tall, red-headed and green-eyed, and all lit up by a crown of bright white light. 'I have to talk to you and Dan,' he said, and they sat quiet and obedient while he spoke.

'Ned will have a child,' he announced, 'but none for Dan.' And, his flare gradually fading, his father described for them a vision of a little girl, long-haired and pretty, swimming in a quiet creek, and she immediately appeared to him too, and he knew that this was his child-to-be. But a dark mass rose abruptly from below the creek's surface, spreading and growing around this paddling child with her straight, streaming hair, and the mass engulfed her and she was gone.

MAYBE I dwell too much on dreams. They say the trouble with the Irish was that they relied too much on dreams and not enough on men and gunpowder.

Whereas the English were shy on dreams as usual but had plenty of the other.

Well, we've got them all.

I have something to say.

I have something to say.

At this stage, ladies and gentlemen, we might remind Mr Curnow to consider that tonight in the Glenrowan Inn, in the warmth and hospitality of the parlour of Ann Jones's pub, he is privileged to be a witness to history. And how many schoolteachers, Mr Curnow, dream of that?

Any moment, when that train arrives from Benalla, the order of things in this country will explode to smithereens and be changed forever. Call it the opening blow.

Eh, Mr Curnow? Mr Stanistreet? And you, of course, Constable Bracken? Won't you join us, gentlemen, in charging your glasses and drinking to the new Australia?

Thank you, Mr Curnow. My spirits exactly. Joe, Dan, please assist Mr Bracken to join the toast. Blast him to his feet if necessary. And then to Kingdom Come.

That's better.

NOW I'M in full flight, the bloody cockatoo won't stop chattering. Old misty-eyed Martin Cherry and his mates are starting up again: Ned, Ned, he's saying your name. Who could tell in all that squawking? Now it's woken up Mrs Reardon's kids. Fixing its warty eye on me, shrewd as a witch. Tongue like a .44 bullet peeping out. The only word I can make out is *bastard*. Grizzling children and drunken fawning smiles everywhere I look.

Jesus, I've got to depend on these people?

Steve picks up my mood — and the cockatoo. He stuffs it in its cage, covers the cage with a coat. Cherry and his mates grumble, the bird flutters but wisely goes quiet.

I have something to say! My friends and Messrs Curnow, Stanistreet and Bracken, your attention please!

Is that a noise? No.

I have an announcement, penned in the quiet of a recent hideout, that I wish to read. Lying low in caves, eating uncooked food, being tracked by blacks and hunted by police, gives you words and aims and concentrates your mind. Listen close and spread the warning wide.

Ahem.

A Statement on Treachery, with Consideration to Recent Events.

By the light that shines, this is my warning:

Being pegged on an ant bed with your belly

opened, fat stripped out, rendered and poured, boiling, down your throat, will seem the coolest of all pleasantries compared to that pleasure of pleasures I will give persons taking blood money from the police.

Fair notice to my enemies. (You know who you are.) Sell out your property, leave the State, give ten pounds of every hundred to the widow and orphan fund.

Neglect this warning and the consequences shall be a thousand times worse than Drought and Grasshopper Plague and Rust in the Wheat.

I am a widow's son outlawed, and my orders Must Be Obeyed.

While God gives me strength to pull a trigger, if my people don't get justice and the innocent aren't released from prison, I'll revenge everything of the human race.

It will pay the Government to give those selectors who are suffering in innocence their justice and liberty. If not, I will open the eyes not only of the police and the people but also the whole British Army. There will be no peace while the police are empowered to arrest a man and refuse him land because of his associates or utterances. I warn the authorities: beware your railroads. *And your coppers and your banks!*

Because the police spies are afraid – or ashamed – to wear their uniforms, so every man's life is in danger from me. As I was outlawed without cause, and cannot be held in worse regard, and as I can only die once, I seek revenge for the evil name given to me and my relations.

Horrible disasters shall follow if Fitzpatrick's lies are not righted. Fitzpatrick shall be the cause of greater slaughter to the rising generation than St Patrick was to the snakes and frogs in Ireland.

If I had robbed, plundered, ravished and murdered everyone I met, my character could not have been painted blacker. But my conscience is as clear as the snow in Peru.

A sweet goodbye from Edward Kelly, a Forced Outlaw.

THANK YOU, thank you, thank you – *How did that go over, Joe?* – Drinks all round, Mrs Jones. And please nail this epistle over the mantelpiece.

'Jane! . . . Now I want a moment's peace to talk to this elegant young lady.'

— If I were game I could just say that.

Or, 'Jane, come outside and take the air with me. Don't you think it smells of jungle?'

Jesus, in gaol all my wild-oat years! Never kissed or touched a woman younger than me. Face so shyly blushed and smooth. So strange and sisterly, seems wrong, but no. I think I'd prefer this less blatant hunger, a mouse's earhole for a change. No more eyes lined with shrewdness, drink and compromise. Those sinews and soft muscles working visibly. She flows, and every move's a dance.

Liquid moves, fresh eyes, shining hair, clear spittle on her tongue, pink gums. This changes things. Jane Jones.

To JANE (*while sauntering, taking the air*) I'll quietly ask: Did you like the part about the ant bed? It came to me while hiding in a cave in the Wombat Ranges. And from an adventure yarn I borrowed from Scott, the Euroa bank manager. (Plus a few other things!) This Apache tribe liked torturing white settlers with ants. They'd stake them out on ant beds in the desert sun. They didn't care to learn their secrets, they just fancied the idea.

Have you heard of that before? With all the ants we've got I think it would work well here. *Ha, ha.*

Lying low like we are now, having to live in caves, you can't help watching ants. (*I'll go on in this vein.*) You learn small creatures' lives. Eventually you can read rocks and soils like books. I've watched gravel fade, dust settle into crust and the second-by-second variations in the shadows. I've seen drips of water turn to stone that defied gravity and reason and assumed the shapes of lacy shawls and giant rashers of bacon. My buttocks (*pardon me*) can clock the different temperature changes in granite and sandstone. True, I can forecast the weather with my arse. (*Whoops!*) I've seen a hundred shades of lichen, the different moisture grades of moss. I've lived so quiet in limestone caves that owls and bats ignored me and spiders were impressed with my calm spiderness.

I've turned blood-red with cave mud until I looked like some underground formation. I've drunk groundwater so full of iron I pissed red. I've *been* a bloody rock.

I've spent a day watching a caterpillar die. Fell from a gumtree onto the rock beside me and I flicked it into a patch of sun among some sugar ants. I could've pushed it into the safety of shade or under a leaf but I was curious about its fate among ants. Well, they were in a frenzy in a second. Do you know that an ant kills a grub like a lion kills an antelope? Jumps on its back and bites it on the neck. Well, this grub twirled and spun in agony, and finally spiralled away into a pile of leaves. But here a new tribe of bigger ants were hunting. They were delighted with their luck but those other ants scurried in a bewildered way. Couldn't get over it. Where's our lovely grub gone?

Sorry for the caterpillar? Funny question. Maybe. *But not enough to save it.*

You know ants panic when a storm is coming? They up stakes and shift their camp. Friday night, the night before Aaron died, they swarmed into our blankets so we knew we were in for a storm. It struck quickly — hailstones like eggs, lightning, fierce winds. Branches splintered and trees toppled over us, roots and all. You could say the ants forecast Aaron getting it.

What do you want to know about that for? A sweet one like you. You knew Aaron? He didn't miss many around here. And now he's got a widow even younger than you.

Well, if you really want to know . . .

WE LIKED the idea of a full moon. So it had to be Saturday 26th June, this weekend. The timing was important. Aaron had to die early in the evening. The rails couldn't be torn up until after the last passenger train passed through Glenrowan at 9 p.m. We expected the police to reach Beechworth with the news of Aaron later than night, and Hare's police special to pass through here this morning, Sunday, the 27th.

That was the plan. Stage One. Well, it's nearly midnight, Sunday. So where is it, Jane? Tell me why it isn't here.

JOE HAD to be the executioner. Aaron was his schoolmate, his gaolmate, almost his brother-in-law.

(I guess we were all that!) Police Agent Sherritt shopped us all to Hare, but it was worse for Joe. They were like brothers, comrades, all the rest. Chased girls together – and caught them too.

It takes a certain type of friendship to share a woman turnabout. A barmaid named Maggie who Joe was slipping out at night to see also caught Aaron out. When Aaron got married and still came bouncing round to see her, Maggie told him she didn't go with married men. Cut him to the quick. This night she knocked him back again, and later in the evening caught him drinking with one of Hare's detectives and glaring in her direction. While Aaron was out relieving himself the detective suddenly asked her about Joe, when she saw him and where. When Aaron came back and saw him questioning her his face went tight and sober and pale around the mouth. He looked like a man who'd made the mistake of his life, Maggie said.

I asked Joe whether it was hard shooting his oldest friend close up like that, in the face and chest.

He said it was easy once he knew for sure. Same as a kangaroo – no, the same as a steer. Someone else's. The taste of blood came into his mouth then too, like he'd bitten his tongue. Warmish and sweet but without the pain.

What had made him angriest was when Aaron started putting on airs and graces with his police money and affecting an accent like a grazier's. He forgot he was just some shitkicker's son like us.

Yes, I guess he's cold enough now to call him Judas. He offered to spy on us. Said he and Joe had been in crime together all their lives. Told Hare our plans, led him to our hideouts, wanted to get us shot or hanged. Take my word for it. Aaron had to go.

Jesus, wanting to be liked by both sides, giving secrets in order to be liked, taking money – how could that work? Hiding behind women's and police-men's skirts and still getting splattered like any soft-eyed roo shot by lamplight.

Aaron's child-bride Mary took the murder very bad. Her mother too. They were both there at the shooting. The four troopers guarding Aaron were quite upset as well, if their muffled pleas from under the bed were any indication.

He and his father were always quarrelling over Aaron's Catholic girlfriends – Joe's sister Kate, my sister Kate too and finally Mary Barry that he married.

Aaron didn't share his old man's Protestant beliefs, or his girls' Catholic ones. Aaron believed only in the moment. Well, he's had his.

BUT THE trouble with killing Aaron was that now he'd never know for sure why he'd done it.

Money was too simple. Their manner the day they rested in his hut at Sebastopol must have got his goat. Their new, no-bullshit, serious-outlaw air. They were stealing a lot of thunder these days and maybe Aaron wanted some limelight too. Plus the Maggie and Joe affair. Half-jealous over fame and sex and then Hare manipulating the rest. Putting ideas in his head. Telling him he was someone.

Just guesswork. But his mother had never trusted Aaron. She was a good judge of men's characters, except when they were after her.

AT NIGHT she pads naked around the crowded, sleeping bodies, softly prowls the brushed-earth floor, the dark maze of the hut. Her wedding ring tings against the water dish, a knee creaks as she squats. A sloshing upward and fainter liquid pattering. Burning in the dark, his eyes feel they must be lighting up the room. His breaths whistle in his nose. It's so quiet the towel rasps against her thighs; she must hear his raw eyes blinking. But she dries herself, then silence. For minutes she's invisible, her outline fading in darkness, then she's standing moonlit, motionless, at the window, staring out into the night. The layers of dark mystery now visible and triangle black on black. And then she starts suddenly – *Ohh!* – at something out there. Something looking in at her.

Her murmur brings a rattling snore from whatsisname. His breath overtakes all air within the hut, his inside gases and sour skin a cloud from wall to roof to floor. Same age as me give or take a couple of years.

Always managing to flash it somehow. Sisters try to turn away, leave the room, but he's onto that. Oh, Kate, Maggie, pass Daddy that towel/vest/shirt/boot/pair of long johns. Pardon old John Thomas, mind of his own, likes to see the light of day now and again. Don't look at me like that, all churchy, we're family now.

She's sluiced you away, boyo! Wiped away your scum.

A big owl gave me a fright last night, she says next morning. Over three feet tall, must be one of those they call a Powerful Owl that can take a cat. It looked in at me and said *Woo-hoo.*

Woo-hoo! he says, grabbing out for her in front of us. *Woo-hoo!*

I'M IN a corner in O'Connell's playing dominoes with Joe and drinking bottled bitter on a gritty afternoon. King weaves up, slaps my back and edges his face into my air. His beard's as neatly tended as a Malvern lawyer's hedge. Flour still in his fingernails and arm hairs. A yeasty smell older than his age. New brandy on his yeasty breath. I hate to look that close at any man's mouth — lips, teeth and coated tongue. The last thing I want to know is a man's gizzard secrets.

'You never come home,' he grizzles like a huffy aunt. 'You never look me up when you're in town.'

He'd thought we could be mates now we're related, work some land together, maybe pan a bit of gold like we did that time at Bullock Creek, sell a few horses. He's oven-crazy, sick of the hours in Rassmussen's bakery, wants the freedom of the outside life again. I don't know whether he's going to sing a ballad or burst into tears.

'Important game in progress,' I say.

'I gave you those steers once I pinched at Blind Man's Gully,' he goes on. 'Called off Detective Ward when he came sniffing round with good bribes to get something fishy on you.' Then he peevishly changes tack. 'I hear you're hitting the grog. Looks like it from your face; anyway, your mother's in a state.'

I swallow a mouthful of ale and turn aside and George M. King yells, 'I'm talking to you!' and backhands the dominoes to the floor. So I swing back with my half-full bottle against his jaw just before his full one arcs around and clubs my ear. As we're thrashing on the ground, Joe's on his knees picking up the dominoes from under us, dusting them off and carefully placing them down, frowning with a watchmaker's precise intent as he tries to remember the order of play.

'These are nice bone ones, ivory or whalesteeth or something similar,' Joe says. 'And I had a natural then, so one of you bastards owes me two pounds ten.'

Sent my stepfather home to Eleven Mile Creek unconscious on his horse, strapped on face to arse to make the point. My head still ringing from his bottle blow, my stomach mainly squeamish with what my mother'll think, I pulled his baker's hat down on him tight against the wind and gave the horse a whack so it wouldn't stop until it reached her, or at least the watch-peacock.

Impossible to tell her of the tart her husband's baking, the assistant pastrycook, the skinny, one-armed girl that lost it above the elbow in the Wangaratta bridge collapse. That I was just counting on a free warm poppyseed loaf when I dropped in at five that morning in that hungover month and heard a familiar accented night-time grunting.

In puffs of flour George King's doughy backside bucked over the blackbutt rolling bench. Amid this dusty flurry her ghostly stick legs angled out. My step-father couldn't see the intruder but she did. But she held me with her stare, eyes like a serious clown's in the floured face, and said not a thing. Somehow made me

someone else, something between witness and accom-
plice. This broken biscuit just stared at me in silence
and clasped him tighter to her with her defiant stump.

ALWAYS ENVIED steady Joe's calmness with the
dominoes.

Another widow's boy, Joe comes and goes around
the countryside, gives his girlfriends baby birds and
melts their hearts. Comes from the Woolshed district
where Reedy Creek runs down to Wangaratta just
north of Beechworth. Grew up on a half-acre clearing,
up against a steep flank of hills. The reason he's footloose was feeling hemmed in by this escarpment as a
boy. His dad Pat died when he was thirteen. Four
girls and two boys. Nice-looking family.

Joe brings the barmaids poddy lambs and calves
he's borrowed from some farmer, and stays the night.
He's the one made up the Kelly Song and over a glass
of Hennessy sings it sweetly in the back bars after
closing time.

See yonder ride four troopers —
One kiss before we part.
Now haste and join your comrades:
Dan, Joe Byrne and Stevie Hart.

He gave Maggie, the barmaid at the Commercial Hotel at Beechworth, a baby curlew. She fed it bread and mincemeat of a morning but it didn't thrive. So Joe would leave our hideout every night to bring it insects and feed it by moonlight like its mother. When he'd arrive he'd sidle up and softly call *Ker-loo!* One palm nestling the feeding bird, the other a Hennessy three-star.

She only asks me one thing, he says of Maggie. Whose horse have you got tonight? Just one of Hare's, I say. Behind the pub in her bedroom made of slabs and lined with paper and hessian against the cold he and the bird would snuggle down and say *Ker-loo!* Revolver nestling in his boot, Joe a night bird too.

What else? To keep so steady and balanced Joe wears on his right hand a topaz ring he took from Scanlon's dead finger, and on his left a gold ring with a white seal from a favourite girl. My calm friend Joe keeps a prayer book in one pocket of his jacket and in the other some .45 bullets and a brown-paper packet marked *Poison*.

STEVE'S SLOWLY shuffling Dan's playing cards. Entertaining old Cherry and his cronies. When he flicks them like that the showgirl seems to be shedding her clothes. Comes out from behind that cheeky parasol, bending and beguiling in her whalebone and frillies.

Good poker cards. Optimistic new players always concentrating on the showgirl on the back of your hand instead of the front of their own. Takes a few games before they realise she's mostly so creased and stained with dirt and cave mud they're lucky to even make out her head.

Steve's caught me looking at my watch again. He's been sulking since Jerilderie, since I made him give back the watch he'd lifted from some clergyman.

No more watches.

That can't be the time. Two o'clock. Well into Monday!

Come and see the lion I captured (*I'll say to Jane*). PREY CAPTURES LION – there's a heading for the *Argus*.

You wouldn't know there was a lion in there? Breathe deeply. Now? Look into the gloom. In that corner – yes, a female. An old lioness. Feel that meaty heat and breath. Those snores are dreams of instinct, memories of cubs grown up or dead, of ancestors killing unknown straight-up things like us.

Do you do this? Sometimes out in the bush, in head-high scrub, I imagine I'm in Africa, hunted by yellow hidden eyes and silent paws. Jaws slobber at my possibilities. What am I, a pale sort of buck, a thin gorilla, a vertical pig? I'm a curious and dangerous smell, sweet and stale at once, a jagged mystery of an outline, but obviously a walking meal.

When a male lion takes over a new pride he kills the cubs of the male before him.

That's how animals see things. Wish I had horns sometimes, sharp hoofs, eyes in the back of my head. Read in a geography book back at the Avenel Common School where the natives of India wear masks behind their heads, big painted eyes facing to the rear. Tigers creeping up on them see these eyes, think they've been spotted and shy off. That's the theory anyway — I'd like to see the figures on backwards-facing tiger dinners.

Got it wrong. I'm one of them. An animal anticipating the hunter's bullet any day and anywhere. Only four men in the country — in the whole Empire — that any citizen's allowed to kill, no questions asked. Guess who? Open season on Ned and Dan, Joe and Steve, and the biggest reward yet offered in the world. It's up to eight thousand pounds.

The Queen said so. Regina versus Us.

SEE THIS ball of lion hair. This cat is rubbing itself to death. It can't live with wanting us so much.

You can plait it, make a keepsake bracelet of it, Jane.

Speaking of Africa, that booking on the ship to Cape Town. The tickets even paid for. Letting it sail from Melbourne without us. Crazy.

— That springy rise and fall of her . . .

Has anyone seen Curnow? Where's he gone? Bloody schoolteachers!

Third night without sleep. I'm a little dizzy. What's this on my hand? Bloody mosquito.

Curnow's gone.

This is one trick we've got up our sleeves. *Armour!* What do you think? A surprise for Hare? Well, we tried both India rubber and ordinary sheet iron before I decided on plough mouldboards. Dressed a tree stump in a vest of India rubber, fired a Winchester at it from twenty yards. Did it pierce the vest? Yes, both sides, and the stump right through as well.

Went through the sheet iron too. Only the front of it and six inches into the stump, but far enough to kill you twice.

Lennon the blacksmith made the jackets from iron cultivators. My sisters sewed the padding. Tested with all weapons and bulletproof at ten yards. Designed to protect the head, body, upper legs and thighs. And of course the family jewels. Too heavy for any police bullets to get near us. My armour weighs ninety pounds, the headpiece alone twenty-five pounds.

Hare won't be able to touch us.

What?

The terrifying absence of a whistle.

Jane hears a noise like a train steaming into a station. Ann Jones hears the squeal of wheels braking. Dan and Steve hear the clatter of horses being unloaded and men's voices and running feet and come running themselves, spilling their drinks. Half the bar suddenly saying they heard something. But no one heard a train whistle, a warning.

No whistle!

Joe says, 'Curnow stopped the train.' And while they go to put on their armour Bracken unlocks the parlour door and escapes to the station.

Joe says, 'Bracken's escaped.'

Everyone hears the noise of the first of them making their way to the pub, the scrambling, crouching running, the scattering, the urgent low voices, sharp erratic hoofbeats. Rifle sounds.

Everyone hears the silence.

He says, hears himself say, 'Put out the lights.' What he's been waiting for, wanting to happen.

Then it starts.

Considering the size and speed of the target, it's a lucky shot someone potting the monkey in the first volley. But this is chaos. 'The monkey's shot,' Joe announces, dragging on his armour. He's unheeding of the bullets spraying through the weatherboards, shattering the windows, sending shards and splinters flying.

The monkey bares its eyeteeth in a spitting screech, then claws and gnaws a frenzied scratching, searching its belly for this demon flea. 'Someone better tell Orlando,' Joe says, as it performs a last desperate backward-somersault onto the rump of some phantom circus pony and rides into oblivion or maybe Africa.

Bottles ping and smash. Dan and Steve clank

together up the corridor through the gloom, police bullets sparking and humming off their armour. They look around. They pull up the bar counter and partitions and barricade the walls with the flimsy furniture. As he adjusts his armour straps Joe softly curses various police by name.

Lying on their faces in the front room, thirty or forty people. The women screaming and pressing into the floorboards, the children sobbing, the men crying out to the police to stop firing, for God's sake. Some pray, or vomit up the weekend's booze, or both. In the corner under the dartboard, wrist still connected to his monkey's chain, Orlando lies snoring on his back. Some panicky farmer's suggesting calling on the police to hold their fire and then all rushing out the door. Some labourer yells that if someone will only give him a gun he'll fucking shoot the lot of them.

Joe says to them all, 'You're better off where you are,' and fires nonchalantly through the window at a glimpse of bearded face.

A woman shaking Orlando awake sees his snoring is really the gurgling effect of the bullet that passed neatly through his eye.

Bleeding from the mouth, Johnny Jones is

moaning in the back room with a bullet through his belly. Ann Jones is wailing and begging nearby men to help her shift her son, but no one is keen to move. At last her roustabout, old Martin Cherry, rises from the floor and they drag the boy under the bar.

There's a towel on the bar for soaking up keg slops. Cherry reaches up for it, to make a pillow for the boy's head, and in stretching embraces a hot ricocheting bullet.

The police keep up the tempo of firing from two sides, bullets crossing in the corridor, bullets cat's-cradling and spinning so the hallway's a buzzing grid.

Jane appears in the front parlour holding a candle, her brother's blood on her. 'All women and children come out with me.' She leads a large party out the back door towards the railway gatehouse.

A voice calls from a drain beside the road, 'Who's coming there?'

'Women and children,' Jane yells. From the drain a burst of shots passes their heads and they break and run for their lives back to the pub.

They run along the verandah and throw themselves into the parlour again as a shot hits the clock on the mantelpiece and sets it striking. It bongs sixty or seventy times before another bullet sends it exploding and uncoiling to the floor and, after it, Cherry's taciturn old cockatoo in its cage.

Over the floorboards mingled fluids trickling now — booze, urine, vomit, human and monkey blood. Every so often Dan or Steve moves to a door or window or into the open air to fire randomly, but mostly they stand in the passage or keep to the room they use as an armoury. Inside their armour they look small and aimless. They're calling out for him.

This is when a bullet enters Jane sideways through the stomach. She jolts, tilts over gracefully on her other side, meets all life's detritus at once, cheek resting in the slops, the dust, the butts, the glass.

Across the paddock, from the shadows behind the big tree stump beyond the lion's wagon, two rockets spurt up — one bright, one faint. The signal. Now we'll see.

HE MUST get through the cordon now and meet them.

He hadn't realised the armour would slow things down so much.

He arrived opposite the station as the last police were pouring off the train. Six Aborigines smoking pipes — the blacktrackers — sidled out of the rear goods van and assembled on the platform in front of a white man in a pith helmet. Just another tree trunk, invisible in the dark, he froze there in front of them until they sloped off. Then an armour bolt wouldn't fit into its bloody slot. *Jesus.* By the time he'd adjusted it the police were firing into the inn. The screaming started. He was halfway back when he got a stray bullet in the foot, another in the left arm.

Only after the third police volley did he and the Gang return fire. He caught sight of a sergeant he knew, Steele, an eager Englishman stationed at Wangaratta who'd hunted him for years. Steele was shooting at the inn like a madman. What a pleasure to aim back at him. Oh, he had to hold the Winchester at arm's length to get a sight. His smashed left arm couldn't support it properly, so he fired it like a pistol, shooting at the flashes of Steele's gun in the clouds of gunpowder smoke. But he couldn't hold it steady and his bullet hit the earth ten feet in front of him.

Then in the smoke he saw Hare arriving just over there, *Hare! Thank Christ*, reloaded (hampered by the armour), aimed a chest shot careful as he could with only one good arm, and shot him in the *hand*. Heard him cry, 'Good gracious, I'm shot!' Saw him leaving – *no!* – saw him shepherded away to safety, saw him disappear into the fog.

SOMEHOW HE'S back by the pub verandah, by the crashing glass and massed shrieking. Waiting. Bullets plopping past him into the wooden walls. People with contorted faces scuttling like mad hens past the lit windows. He's shouting again, 'Put out the lights and lie down!' Still they're crisscrossing and blubbing. His voice is deafening, reverberating inside the helmet, but no one seems to hear. A film comes and goes like skin across his eyes, his breath booms like a boiler in his ears.

Joe's standing quietly near the back door in the darkness. He's removed his helmet and is leaning on the bullet-pitted doorframe. Now the first barrage seems to be lessening. Only desultory bullets patter through the front wall of the pub. You can hear the lion again. 'We could take off,' Joe says.

He shakes his head. He says he's signalled the Peak contingent. They'll be here any moment now. The Mob, their friends, his Mick soldiers. He must go and meet them, lead them in.

He moves off into the smoky dark, rolling with the armour weight, boots crunching frosty gravel. The frost is clamping down the mist and gunsmoke clouds close to the ground. Bullets snaking low, hissing through the dewy grass. Some shots nick his boots. Someone shoots him in the chest. It ricochets off. He shoots back into the fog and disappears into it himself. Fierce police fire starts up again and – can it be possible? – an even greater pitch of screaming.

MOONLIGHT PIERCING the cold smoke. Acrid milky blue tendrils reaching around trees and men and the heads of frightened horses pulling on their tethers. He can just pick out a white handkerchief. A prisoner is waving a white handkerchief out of the pub's parlour window. Immediately it's hit by bullets. Dan's voice tells the shaking woman waving the handkerchief, Emma Reardon, that she must get her children out.

'Make them scream, and scream yourself,' Dan yells.

She does. She steps out onto the verandah, screaming. Her children screaming.

From the blue mist beyond the verandah, an arm with a gun, a face, appear. 'Hands up or I'll shoot you like bloody dogs,' Sergeant Steele says.

Emma Reardon tucks her baby under one arm, raises the other and steps off the verandah, followed by her husband Dick and four more children. Steele fires into the family. A bullet scorches into the baby's blanket. Panicked, Dick turns back with the kids. Steele fires again at the woman. When she falls he shouts, 'I've shot Mother Jones in the bum!' Then he orders the oldest Reardon boy to throw up his arms, and shoots him through the shoulder. 'I've wounded Dan Kelly!' yells mad ecstatic Steele.

Coming and going, lumbering and invisible, deflecting and absorbing bullets – he may as well be made of smoke – he sees all this. He sees especially an empty moonlit sky above the Peak. Still no answering flare. No silhouettes of men on horses coming down the slope. Beyond the pub the police train sits at the railway station, then empty fields and bush spread back to the silent hills.

Joe too is watching the general scene from the verandah. Not bothering to shoot now, bullets pinging off him. He goes into the back bar and asks how everyone is. Then he strides up to the bar, rests his rifle on the counter and pours himself a tumbler of whisky. Puts a foot up on the bar rail. *Fuck this for a joke.* Takes a swig, notices his foot up on the rail allows the smallest gap — what, half an inch, three-quarters? — to open between the armour plates. *So what?* And a single bullet zips into the room and precisely through the gap in the armour without even tipping metal and rips into his groin. He raises the glass for a toast, frowns as if considering what's appropriate when fate's bullet has burst your balls through the only gap in your armour, through the femoral artery, blood already pounding and fountaining like Aaron's. Well, this will have to do. 'Many more years in the bush for the Kelly Gang,' Joe cries, spins around twice, topples and dies in the clanging fall.

Steve and Dan are staring out. Dan seems to have the shivers. What now? They've stopped shooting at the police. All Dan is doing is calling for him, there but not there, in and out of the fog. Abruptly Dan takes off his helmet and whistles his dog out, c'mon boy, coaxes it, trembling, from under the bar, crouches down, who's my old boy, pushes his face against the muzzle, the dry nose, dry jowls, inhales dry dog breath, my old boy then.

Wants the dog to breathe more on him, fill his lungs, smother him in breath and slobber. Hugs the dog so hard it yelps and pulls away.

Out there Sergeant Steele is still shooting. Now he decides, good idea to shoot their horses to prevent a getaway. Picks them off one by one. In a lather now. Doesn't stop after four, shoots all the local horses within range, all the prisoners' screaming nags, then the circus ponies too, and five shots into the camel — two head, three hump shots, sounds like shooting sheepskin rugs on the clothesline — just in case.

Thank God he's hidden Mirth behind the saplings, removed her from all this.

Steele's running up to the circus wagon. He's

wearing a deerstalker hat, brogues, leggings. He's poking his rifle through the bars, shooting the lioness roaring in her fear — shooting her!

ONLY WAY to end all this is to find Hare. *Understand you've been looking for me. Here I am. Stop this business or we're both dead — you first.* So, turning back through the blur to the railway station, the special police train — and surely this is fantasy now.

Women in dressy clothes and reporters are helping Hare on to the platform and into the V.I.P. carriage. *The officers have brought their ladies on this outing! He can't get near him.* Hare is pale and brave while the ladies fuss with bandages. Trussing up his sore wrist for him. Opening a picnic hamper and helping him to some sherry through the window. The reporters shouting to the engine driver to hasten him and his wound to Benalla for treatment.

He's leaving. The engine getting up steam. The ladies, too, suddenly deciding it might be best to leave this dangerous troublespot, and climbing aboard. The engine shunting towards Wangaratta, then reversing and disappearing rapidly with the ladies, leaving Hare's unconnected and stationary carriage behind.

He's immobilised watching this circus. Giddy at the sight of Hare indignantly quaffing sherry. Reporters rallying around his carriage window, the gentlemen of the press shouting for a pilot engine to come and pick him up. The pilot shunting up and laboriously connecting with Hare's carriage. Hare finally disappearing, his white and noble profile framed in the carriage window, Hare chasing after the rest of the train, leaving the scene, off to the doctor's, joining the ladies, *chuff-chuff.*

Why are parrots pecking his shins? Lorikeets scaling his legs, parakeets dancing up his calves, hanging from his kneecaps. Feathery body heat rustling in his pants legs worse than mice. Hot beaks nibbling at his veins, claws gripping. Any deeper and they'll be pecking his bone marrow. Creeping up and ripping his foreskin off, Holy Mother! In the rising light he gets to his feet, whacks and whacks his shins with his rifle butt to smash the little pecking parrots.

The agony brings him round but bashing his legs has made them bleed again from shin to thigh where they're peppered with shot. They've also picked up bullets on his treks back and forth across the lines. The blood loss from the wound in his left arm has turned it numb and both arms are pocked with shot as well. He's soaked with dew.

Dawn is coming but the glen around the pub still lies in foggy shadow. Intermittent shots still bring moans and occasional screams. The native birds are silent but, tentatively, a rooster crows.

Once more, slowly, he rounds the hotel to the back. Dan's voice, raw and high, still calls for him. Time to get the boys out, although the way they just stood there giggling and farting when the eagle tried to carry him off before, just lounged there cackling, still makes him angry. Can't rely on anyone. He'll have words later.

He raps on his breastplate with his revolver butt and calls their names. Dan's dog hears his voice and barks. At this noise the police step up their shooting again. Dan peers out. 'Joe got it in the balls,' he says.

Now he's dreaming, standing. Dreaming of being shot himself, of shattering into a thousand pieces. While he's propped, feet apart for balance, to support the great weight on him, his soul's iron burden, new bullets pop and zing around him, at him, hit him. Somewhere a dog is barking. A dog's head is poking through the side of the hut, as if the wall were

194

air, snout and black lips curling inches from his face. (Joe's snoring, oblivious, in the next bunk. Where is this, Bullock Creek?) Hello, boy. Why's the dog's pointed muzzle wrinkled in this snarl of the greatest evil? Long teeth edging closer. Fear cold as a knife blade flat against his neck.

Listen to me, his mother says, they've all got it wrong. It's not you that's the very devil, truly, this is it. Shoot the dog.

Muzzle to muzzle, he shoots and the blast turns it to air.

Talking to her in his head like this, concentrating so deeply, he gets a tingling in his scalp and forehead that fills his skull. This is hard work, he says to her, sounds like a gulf roaring in my prickly head. One more thing, am I playing at being dead, or am I?

It's not him that is. In the back room of the pub it's Dan and Steve lying side by side full-length on the floor with bags rolled up under their heads for pillows and their armour laid to one side. Beside Dan lies his dog, also shot through the head.

THE BONFIRE they danced around, he and Jane, comes in handy. When, after three hours, some officer finally decides the surviving prisoners can leave the pub, and the last sobbing woman has reached the police lines, a nervous constable rushes up and grabs a torch from the embers, and scrapes up some dry grass and gum leaves, and in a few minutes smoke and flames are rising from the splintered weatherboards of the verandah.

They think he's inside. He sees the flames engulf the pub and turns away. With difficulty he stands. He advances. Stamps through the weeds behind the burning inn, revolver in his right hand, his left hand hanging. Sun well up and glaring. His armpits running with some moisture, his thighs, this copious seepage from his iron skirt. Surely he didn't piss himself. Where's Mirth?

Mirth passes by in an aimless canter, reins trailing. He tries to whistle her, turns after her, and Steele is in his shadow, running up behind, swinging his twelve-bore like a club. He points the revolver at Steele but nothing happens that he notices except that Steele is now aiming point-blank at his knees. Steele firing again at his hands, his legs, peppering his extremities, undermining him with swanshot, tipping him. He's pealing like a church bell full of hornets. Sun piercing his eyes as he spins. The inevitability of this final jolt to brain and spine, the jarring clamour of turning turtle.

There is a loud intake of breath from the crowd as one of the blacktrackers drags Joe's body out on to the smouldering verandah. Joe is hardly burnt at all, just a little smudged. There's a train at the station. The crowd begins to mutter as the police roll Joe onto a plank, carry him to the train and push him into the guard's van. There is shouting. Hundreds of local farmers, railway workers and people from nearby towns are pressing against the police cordon around the pub and moving around the stationmaster's room where they're guarding him. He recognises faces trying to peer through the window.

When the blacktrackers rake out Dan's and Steve's remains there is a deep gasp, then a sweeping '*Ohhh!*' By now the Mob has defined its attitude. 'They're ours!'

the Mob cries of these charred lumps not more than three feet long, not recognisably human. It surges forward and tries to take the bodies from the police. *'They're ours! They're ours!'* Men are struggling, women too. Fights are breaking out. The police size up the situation and surrender them. The lumps are wrapped tenderly in blankets and quickly spirited away.

A doctor treats him while his bleeding wrists and ankles are tied. A priest hears his confession and anoints him. Maggie and Kate are allowed to kiss him. Then four police carry him on to the train for Benalla. Six more with drawn pistols guard him, around them another ten with rifles.

Before they set off the fireman comes down for a stickybeak at his notorious passenger. Seeing the sooty face peering at him, he starts as if from a nightmare. As if the creature had come to drag off his burned body. 'Send the devil away,' he says.

When he next opens his eyes an officer is looking down at him. The bottom half of the carriage window is purple ranges streaming past, drifting leached-grey trees; the top half is white sky. The officer pours himself a brandy, then pours him a shot and holds it for him while he sips. 'You're ours,' he says.

They want him looking like an authentic outlaw but Joe's refusing to hold a pistol for them, keeps dropping it on the ground.

All day Joe's been outside in the street, busy with the latest trainload of photographers from Melbourne. The pressmen have persuaded the police to hang his body from a pulley in front of the police station in a manner intended to simulate life. A rope around his chest and under his arms is hidden by his jacket. The difficulty is in getting his feet just touching the ground. They don't want him looking as if he's, well, *hanging*. All day they've been laughing and bantering and hoisting Joe up and down the wall to get him standing just right.

In the Benalla lockup they've put Joe and him in

adjoining cells. When he woke, Christ, there was Joe propped up on the bunk, winking, one eye open and looking straight at him through the bars. A draught from the corridor ruffling his hair. A bemused and pleasant expression on his face, arms bent stiffly in front of him as if he was carrying a heavy load of firewood inside or as if his hands were sore. (He's slightly singed about the fingers.) A little self-conscious about his black-crusted pants.

Long shadows falling. Any moment now they'll have to pack up their tripods and cameras. Soon they'll bring stiff Joe back into his cell. Well, he's done his dreaming but it's a long night ahead.

Bear with me, Jane, I ramble. These were well-laid plans and I want to do them justice, capture the mood and describe them right.

As I said, a storm blasted down from the Woolshed Hills. This was only two or three days ago but already seems an age away. Anyway, we took its violence as an omen, a clearing of the sullen air, fresh days ahead. The moon, as you can see now, was approaching the full. The Broken River south of town was brimming from the storm. Everything was — is — on our side.

We made our final plans in a shack off the Yackandandah Road. People and supplies arrived. My sisters sewed the linings for our armour. We tried out our new guns at targets. I sent Steve riding off to pass the word to our friends that we were ready. (I can't mention names, you understand.) Dan and his dog stood on a hill keeping an eye on everyone who came and went. Joe? Joe was pretty calm.

AUTHOR'S NOTE

This book is about a man whose story outgrew his life. Although it concerns some people who did exist and touches on actual events, it is a chronicle of the imagination. It owes more to folklore and the emotional impact of some photography and paintings like the famous Victorian photographer John William Lindt's *Joe Byrne's Body on Display at Benalla* and Sidney Nolan's *Ned Kelly* series than to the bristling contradictions of historians and biographers.

I drew on the *Cameron Letter* and the *Jerilderie Letter*, both written or at least composed by Kelly (with Byrne's help), and now held by the Public Records

Office of Victoria, as an indication of Kelly's feelings of persecution.

Other insights came particularly from *The Inner History of the Kelly Gang and Their Pursuers*, by J.J. Kenneally, Moe, Victoria, 1929; *Australian Son*, by Max Brown, Sydney, 1948; and *The Kelly Outbreak 1878–1880: The Geographical Dimension of Social Banditry*, by John McQuilton, Melbourne, 1979.

The paragraph on page 50 about the corpse fostering anxiety paraphrases a saying attributed to André Malraux.

I would especially like to thank my wife Candida Baker for her constant encouragement as well as her invaluable assistance on equine matters.

R.D.

FOR THE BEST IN PAPERBACKS, LOOK FOR THE